FBI Agent Hayes's friend Thomas is kidnapped by a group of six men, trained and heavily armed. Though his wife watches the crime, her observation doesn't result in arrests. Her description reveals though that a crime syndicate operates in the Washington, DC, area, kidnapping young men and taking them to an unknown hideout. Raiden Stout, Lesley's friend, becomes one of the victims, and Agent Hayes joins the investigation to solve the crime and find his friends.

While the FBI agents Hayes and Beckham try to get leads on the kidnappers, more men are abducted, revealing the actions of a crime syndicate. The chase turns into a race against time.

Barred Doors
Copyright © 2021 Ann Raina
ISBN: 978-1-4874-3190-7
Cover art by Martine Jardin

Published by eXtasy Books Inc or
Devine Destinies, an imprint of eXtasy Books Inc

Look for us online at:
www.eXtasybooks.com or www.devinedestinies.com

Barred Doors
Nick and Jacklyn 6

By

Ann Raina

DEDICATION

Your train of thought, my wonderful muse, runs at the same speed as mine. It's great that you're still at my side, mulling over ideas, laughing about silly moments, and enjoying our work together.

CHAPTER ONE

Thomas Zutarski, ATF agent for ten years and husband for five months, lovingly rearranged the wedding photograph on the nightstand. He changed the linens in the bedroom, looking forward to Charlene returning from her visit with Vernon and Teresa Freeman. Now that his wife was six months pregnant, she didn't leave the house alone anymore, and he was glad for her friendship with his superior's wife. Teresa took her to the hairdresser, accompanied her shopping for maternity clothes, and invited her for nights at the movies. She claimed that Charlene needed to go out more often in hope that she would learn to trust other people and live a life of happiness. So far, Charlene took her strength from Thomas and was a nervous bundle the moment he wasn't around to protect her. Thomas believed that the baby would help Charlene look more positively at the world around her. There were times when he thought that taking Charlene away from her former home had been a mistake. She was a girl from a rural town in Virginia and so far had been unable to cope with living close to Washington, DC.

He finished his work, took the laundry to the bin, and fetched a glass of water from the kitchen. He was about to check for a message from Charlene when the phone rang. He laughed picking up. "Hey, Nick, it's kind of you to call. I know I promised to call you, but you know how it is. I hardly had an hour at home. Do you want to come to my place tomorrow around eight or eight-thirty? I bet Charlene will do one of her great pastries."

1

"So there's less booze and more food? I'm game."

Thomas laughed. "Well then, that's settled."

"Bet that I'll be hungry."

"Oh, I know *The night . . .has an appetite*." He laughed when Nicolas groaned. "You know me — the movie man."

"We should send you to a TV show — the man who knows five hundred taglines."

"That would be fun. See you tomorrow." Thomas liked Nicolas, friend and FBI agent, more and more. Their friendship had started while they were both investigating the illegal activities of the Turner family in a small town in Virginia and grew when they fled together and brought members of three big criminal families to justice. When Thomas took a bullet on the run, Nicolas helped him to safety. The weeks they had shared, working as well as suffering, revealed similar character traits and created a bond they maintained and strengthened. Usually, they met twice a month for a chat and a few drinks at a bar in Washington, DC, but due to Charlene's condition, Thomas preferred staying home. He considered himself lucky that Nicolas didn't complain that their *men's night* was no longer a private one.

Thomas put down the phone, smiling and looking forward to their meeting. On the spur of the moment, he took down notes for his weekly grocery shopping, then he heard a strange sound at the back door — rubber boots on stone. When he went toward the door, a hard object thudded against it. Thomas turned around to fetch his gun from the drawer. Simultaneously, the front and back door exploded into a thousand splinters and glass shards. In the quiet night, the noise was deafening. Stunned, Thomas gaped at the hole that had been a solid back door and the three men on each side invading his house. He reached for the phone on the counter, but it was too late. He looked into the muzzles of submachine guns, held by men in combat gear with night vision goggles. Judging by their aggressive approach, they were willing to shoot him if he made a false move.

"Drop it and put your hands behind your head!"

He couldn't fight and win against six armed men, so he did as ordered but checked left and right for a chance to wrest the weapon from the man standing next to him. It galled him that they had surprised him so easily.

"What do you want from me?"

The man to his right swiveled the weapon around to hit Thomas's stomach with the butt. "Shut up!"

Thomas gasped and doubled over.

The attacker stepped out of reach while two others closed in, kept Thomas upright, and put a leather belt around his waist. In a minute, Thomas's wrists were locked in shackles and his hands were covered by an additional leather strap and thus rendered useless. *Why would kidnappers in combat gear use medical restraints? It doesn't make sense.*

He had trouble speaking. "Who are you? Where are you taking me?"

Instead of an answer, Thomas was gagged and blindfolded.

Helpless, he was led out of the house. Upon a barked command, a powerful engine came to life. One of the men pushed Thomas into the cargo area of a van and pressed him onto a bench. A kidnapper locked a collar around his neck that was fastened with a chain to the van's wall. Thomas choked when he moved his head.

"Sit tight, don't make a fuss. It's a long ride."

The van left the curb quickly but without squealing tires. Thomas's only hope rested on a few neighbors who might've noticed the unusual nocturnal ruckus outside their gardens.

Teresa parked her car a block away from Thomas's house to

take a walk with Charlene. The young woman needed exercise and was unwilling to walk alone. It took Teresa a lot of coaxing to get her out of the car and down the sidewalk. Charlene was like a lamb that feared being taken to the slaughterhouse. No matter how often they walked together, Charlene didn't become confident that she lived in a safe neighborhood with friendly people who greeted each other across the fences. A part of her anxiety resulted from the fact that she had led a sheltered life in Florence Town. Another part developed from the knowledge that Tyrone Turner was still at large. In spite of police efforts, the criminal son of the Turner family stayed hidden. Thomas had mentioned Tyrone's connections to a Mexican drug cartel and that he'd left the country to escape trial. A gangster like him, so Thomas said, would seek refuge with other gangsters. Teresa didn't know whether the statement had substance or was meant to soothe Charlene's fearful mind.

Teresa linked arms with Charlene and pulled her forward playfully. "I bet your Mr. Wonderful prepared a snack for you and will carry you upstairs later."

Charlene lowered her chin. Her voice was soft, as always. "He does a lot for me. He's waiting on me hand and foot all day." She let out a deep sigh. "I don't know what I'd do without him. I know, I know, you told me frequently that I'm a strong person and that everything's okay with the baby, but I know—deep in my heart—that Thomas is the solid foundation on which I'm standing."

"Yep, you found one of the good ones. He's—" She stopped and pushed Charlene off the sidewalk behind a row of large bushes that provided cover. "Be quiet," she said when Charlene was about to ask for a reason. "There's someone at your house."

Her eyes were wide as she crouched like a bird ducking behind a bush. "What? Who?"

"Sssh." Teresa peeked at the street. Two men in black gear escorted a handcuffed and blindfolded man toward a gray van, opened the back doors, pushed him in, and clambered up behind him. When the other four men were on board, they closed the doors from the inside. Every move looked rehearsed. They were obviously untroubled by possible witnesses. The van drove off immediately. She squinted to read the license plate, but it was too dark. The van rounded the next corner, and Teresa breathed again.

"What happened?" Charlene wanted to know. She panicked when Teresa didn't answer. "Tell me! What happened?"

Heart beating in her throat, Teresa took her cell phone and called the police and her husband.

It was a long ride without food or water or a stop to relieve himself. The van stopped one time, but only for a few minutes to change drivers. Thomas suffered in the growing heat. He couldn't lie down and was weak and tired when the van finally reached its destination. The collar was unlocked and Thomas was pulled out to stand on wobbly legs. He inhaled deeply, trying to determine the location. The air was much warmer than in Washington, DC, in October. The ride must have taken him southwest. The air smelled of sand, but also of diesel, different kinds of food, and faintly of leather. He heard voices echoing from walls as the men marched him across a large yard. At the entrance of the hall, the floor changed from sand to stone. The smell of mold and old clothes added to the strange mix. Thomas tried to memorize every corner they took to create a mental picture of the building in case he had a chance to escape.

He stumbled, fell on his knees, and was put back on his feet by strong hands. They climbed a flight of stairs. He heard faint murmuring and the sound of running water. Once more, Thomas was aware of his thirst and hunger.

"Stop!"

In front of him, a metal door was opened, squealing in its hinges as if unused for ages. He was pushed forward, then pressed down on his knees.

"Hold still or you stay like this."

Thomas held still while the handcuffs and the belt were unfastened. The men retreated and the door banged shut. A key was turned in the lock, then the heavy steps, as well as the men's mumbled conversation, abated.

Thomas fumbled with the clasp for the gag and ripped off the blindfold. He opened his eyes and thought he was blind. The darkness around him was complete, impenetrable, as if a thick blanket had been drawn over his face. He was kneeling on a hard surface, and the cold stone sucked away his body heat. He got up slowly, carefully. Around him, the air had a musty stench, mixed of men's sweat, unwashed clothes, and excrement. Thomas heard the deep rumble of machines and—further away—metal banged on metal, followed by harsh shouts. Careful not to bump into an obstacle, Thomas stretched out his hands and felt his way forward. He reached cold metal after three short steps, felt along the wall, and found out he was locked in a cell of no more than eight square yards without any windows, resembling a vault. He could stand, but the ceiling was about a yard above his head. Having explored the meager contents of the cell—a metal bucket with water, an empty one, and a thin mattress—Thomas drank and tried to sort out what happened to him. *This is the weekend they didn't play golf.*

The operation had been planned to the last detail. Thomas assumed the kidnappers had waited for nightfall and taken it as an advantage that he had come back to the kitchen. Because of their equipment, they had known he was alone at that time. The kidnappers were trained and disciplined, ordered by someone with military background and money. The equipment was expensive. He couldn't answer the *who* and *why* of his kidnapping, but hoped that someone would show up, even if he was just bragging about how easy it had been to catch an ATF agent.

Nicolas looked out of the window when a black van slowed at the curb to back up onto the driveway of their home. The side displayed the logo of Lesley's *Cave of Love*, her dungeon in Washington, DC. "Tell me, Jacky, did you order a catering service, or did Lesley have problems and take the company car?"

"No, not that I know of." She joined him to watch Lesley get out, wearing tight leather jeans and a midriff top that would make any man turn his head. She waved, grinning happily, prior to opening both back doors. "This is getting interesting. Oh, my . . . no, no, I know what she's doing."

"She bought another piece of furniture for us?" Nicolas made a sound of appreciation. The spanking bench in their private dungeon had been a house-warming gift of a special kind.

"That's not it." Jacklyn hurried toward the door. "Do you remember Raiden?"

"I wondered where he was." Nicolas's eyes widened. "Did she put him in the cargo area?"

Lesley had opened a steel bar door within the van, locked a ramp, and let out her new pet, dressed in black leather tethers with several steel accessories that kept him on all fours. The mittens and knee covers added to the illusion that the dungeon queen had brought her lion on a leash. Raiden appeared at ease, though he was restricted like a hardcore criminal. The gag shaped like a bone was the icing on the cake.

Nicolas heard Jacklyn laugh as she greeted her best friend,

but she also told them to hurry to avoid shocking the neighbors.

Lesley's warm laughter echoed in the hallway. "Oh, you think they'd be shocked? Don't you go for a walk with your sub from time to time?"

Jacklyn put her hands on her hips and looked from Lesley down to Raiden and back. "When I invited both of you for a second breakfast, I expected you to come as a couple—both upright and dressed like normal people."

"Oh. Normal people. Ouch." Lesley's face fell as she became aware that Nicolas was dressed in a dark blue dress shirt and sand-colored pants—upright and without any shackles. She looked contrite. "My bad." She patted Raiden's brown wavy mane. "Before you get this wrong—Raiden was thrilled by my idea to tie him up like this. Okay?"

Jacklyn shrugged. "So, it's three plates and a bowl?"

They burst into laughter once more. Nicolas looked at the guy on the floor. In addition to the many restrictions and a wagging rubber tail in his ass, he was wearing a cock cage that must hurt. The sight made Nicolas's penis ache.

"Do you think it's possible to peel him out of the layers of cuffs and tethers?" Jacklyn cocked her head, the sparkle of joy still in her eyes. "Or did you forget the keys?"

"Keys are old-fashioned. The modern locks are magnetic." Once more, she patted Raiden, who waited patiently, as if kneeling on the floor in the buff was the best thing that ever happened to him. "All right, you win." She turned to Nicolas. "You're about the same size. Would you mind lending him something to wear?"

"Not at all. I prefer four plates instead of three and also the chance for a conversation."

"You're both drags," Lesley complained, making a face. "But, hey, if you're that kind of conservative . . ." The last word sounded like a curse.

Nicolas knew she wasn't angry or annoyed. Lesley preferred to live her life as a dominatrix to the fullest, and that included exotic behavior that *normal people* didn't comprehend. As the owner of several sex shops and a dungeon, she spent more time in leather than a cow.

Jacklyn offered to help her, so Nicolas took his time to set the table and brought the coffee pots when Raiden entered the dining room, pushing back his long hair with both hands. His full beard was short-cropped, emphasizing rather than covering his angular chin. He grinned, as if his entry as a human pet had been the entertainment of the day. Nicolas wondered whether Raiden was ever embarrassed about anything.

They shook hands. "Raiden Stroud." He smoothed the white polo shirt that stood in contrast to his olive skin. "Thanks for the clothes. Les really didn't bring anything for me. She was convinced this would be like a session, only *out of the house.*" He smacked his lips, radiating a kind of relaxation and ease that surprised Nicolas. Though Raiden was in his early twenties, he behaved like a man twice his age — self-confident in a casual way. "But it's better this way."

"I agree." Nicolas was astonished at the fit of his clothes. Even the pants looked like Raiden had bought them. "Let's sit down. Coffee?"

"Better than water and dog chow on the floor."

Nicholas couldn't keep the disgust off his face.

Raiden laughed. With a hearty slap on Nicolas's shoulder he said, "Hey, I'm an easygoing guy. I'd have played the role and loved it. She wasn't lying when she said I agreed to the show. Now it's a different one, but that's also okay. So, yes please, coffee! Buckets, if you have 'em!"

Nicolas handed him a full cup. "So you enjoy being a pet?"

Raiden drank and put down the cup carefully, as if it would break in his big hand.

Nicolas marveled at the tattoos along both arms — tribal

signs and intricate patterns woven like wristbands but no names of loved ones.

"Yes. If the question is about more than me walking around in the buff, though I admit it was quite cold outside, let me tell you something. Before I met Lesley, I'd already been into bondage. I had met many weirdos, who claimed they couldn't live their lives among all the normal boring people, but I never thought that I needed it that much. I changed my mind during the last year. If you ask me what I want—I'd be Lesley's pet twenty-four-seven if it was possible. It's not right now, but I'm working on it."

He paused, but went on when Nicolas didn't say a word. "I need to work for a living, and if I have it right, she's not yet ready for a permanent D/s relationship. I'd like to go home with her. So far, that's off limits." He looked around, breathing deeply. "You live with your mistress. How do you play?" Twitching his brows, he pointed at Nicolas's clothes. "Obviously, you don't have to display your skin all the time."

Nicolas sipped coffee and took his time to answer. "Jacky and I have an arrangement. We're a couple—a normal, even boring couple with normal jobs. If we want to play, we do it in our spare time. This means we aren't striving for a twenty-four-seven setting."

Raiden lowered his chin, and Nicolas read amusement in his amber eyes. His voice was a low, warm humming. "If I'm not mistaken, your mistress would like to expand this *spare time arrangement*. But I'm just the pet." He sipped coffee and looked smug.

Nicolas took a deep breath. With the hint of a smile, he nodded. "Maybe, yes. We . . . had our differences when it came to the hours I give up control. But we settled that."

Raiden's bushy brows twitched.

"We spent fantastic weekends on vacation, mostly filled with playtime." Nicolas sighed, remembering the infamous first weekend when Jacklyn had introduced him to a wide arsenal of shackles, whips, and floggers. He had seen many items for the first time in his life, and many of them gave him the creeps. "But back here — when we have to work — it's not a suitable arrangement. I don't want to come home and change from my suit into shackles. She respects my wishes and wouldn't force me to do anything I hadn't agreed to before."

"If you don't mind me asking . . . you don't sound like a submissive who was out for a new dominant partner. Is it possible that you had no experience until you met her?"

Nicolas played with his napkin. "Not the normal development, huh?"

"That's not what I'm saying. I knew quite early that I thrive on pain combined with sex, so my path was laid for me. The first time I went to a dungeon I was twenty-one, because that's the required age. The lady explained to me that I'm the typical masochistic guy with extras." He looked Nick straight in the eyes. "You didn't know she was a dominatrix when you met her, right?"

Nicolas was torn between enjoying the possibility of speaking freely about his relationship and frustration that Raiden saw through him so easily.

"No." He laughed. "When I met her for the first time, I thought she was a rich prig from a wealthy family and totally out of reach for me."

"Wow." He slapped Nicolas's shoulder, grinning broadly. "And now look at you — you're the servant of that rich prig and grant her power over your body. I bet she's getting off the moment she ties you someplace." Raiden bent to him and lowered his voice. "Does she ask you to struggle as if you didn't want to be tied up?"

Nicolas couldn't hide his surprise, and Raiden nodded like an old teacher, still grinning happily.

"Yeah, yeah, that's the ladies. You could keep them from tethering you, and when you submit, they want you to pretend that you resent being tied."

Nicolas shrugged. "The reward is great."

This time, Raiden's surprise was genuine. "She lets you come every time?"

"Not every time, but I get my share. It's the uncertainty that makes it special."

"But you're allowed to come more than, say, once a month?"

Nicolas hadn't thought about keeping count of his sex life. He shrugged. "I guess so."

"And she has sex with you—in the meaning of—" He wiggled his brows.

"I get the meaning. Yes, we're a couple, as I pointed out. That includes more than being whipped and chained."

As if this was a new concept to him, Raiden wiped his beard and drank coffee. "I guess I should talk with my mistress."

"I guess you're eager to be gagged again," Nicolas warned quietly.

Jacklyn and Lesley joined them at the table.

To adjust to the atmosphere of the gathering, Lesley had borrowed a pink top and jeans from Jacklyn. She sat down, making a face. "Don't say a word. I know I look boring. I even feel boring. These clothes—bah!"

Jacklyn grinned, looking much younger than her thirty-eight years. Nicolas enjoyed her good mood. Both their weeks had been stressful. This Sunday was the reward, meant for spending time together and enjoying life.

"You look perfect, my dear friend, for a nice Sunday morning."

"Oh, now you're ruining it," Lesley replied, rolling her eyes pitifully.

The others laughed, then turned to coffee, bread, and pancakes.

When she poured the fourth cup of coffee, Jacklyn asked, "What do you do when you're not clad in leather and steel?"

"I'm a boat designer." Raiden sounded proud. "Customers come to me and tell me what they want, and I make it possible."

Nick got up to fetch a new milk pot from the refrigerator. "What're we talking about? Fishing boats? Yachts?"

"Yachts, mostly. About seventy feet long, equipped with everything the customer desires."

Jacky beamed at him as she folded her hands under her chin. "So, you're a Genie."

"So to speak." Raiden nodded his gratitude. "And my partner takes care that I don't give away the boats for peanuts. I'm not a businessman, he is. Paul joins the discussion when the customer's already hooked and wants the boat. He's happy and doesn't want to alter his design. That way, Paul makes him pay." He linked his fingers behind his head, grinning. His bicep muscles stretched the cloth. "I can't complain. He makes decent money for all of us on the team."

Nick sat down again. "Clever."

Raiden shrugged casually. "Paul was a bank manager, but then fulfilled his dream of a company. I was just the one he found who was able to build a boat."

"So you studied . . . what? Design?"

"It's called naval architecture. With me came a team of three men, equally qualified. Paul was just the one we needed to handle the finances. It's a win-win situation. Along the coast, there're always rich people who want a new and big boat."

"Sounds like a great job," Jacklyn admitted, then turned to Lesley. "Hmm, what about you? A yacht with the company's name? A swimming dungeon?"

Lesley shuddered. "No one gets me on a boat. Water and I don't go together." She looked around the table and lifted her hands. "Before someone asks—yes, I can swim. No, I haven't had any bad experience in the water, but it ruins my hairdo, my makeup, my skin. If I go swimming, it has to be for emergency reasons—like saving someone from drowning."

Nicolas glanced at Raiden and saw his face fall. If he had hoped to take her on a cruise, the idea sank to the ocean's bottom at that moment.

CHAPTER TWO

Getting up, Lesley pointed at Jacklyn. "Since you ruined my innovative session and if you" — she moved her finger in Nicolas's direction — "want your clothes back, we meet at my dungeon at five for a session. No objection!" she warned Nicolas, who was about to protest. "You can have your own room if you want, my shy G-man, but that's about it."

Nicolas refrained from telling her that he would never in his lifetime agree to a four-person session. Instead, he got up and cleared the table with Raiden.

"You don't look so thrilled," Raiden said quietly as they busied themselves in the kitchen. "Would you prefer to stay home?"

"I know that Jacky loves to play at the dungeon. The possibilities are endless. It would be cruel to deny her wish."

"You're a strange sub." Raiden grinned broadly as he put ham and jelly back into the refrigerator. "But tell me — you have sex with her? I mean, real intercourse? Regularly?"

"I already pointed out that we're living in a relationship. There's love involved and sex, yes."

"How does she treat you?"

Nick stopped sorting dishes into the dishwasher. "Raiden, this is going way too far. As I see it, your relationship is still developing, while mine has grown over three years. You have to be patient. So far, you seemed satisfied with what you have."

"Satisfied? Sometimes, yes. She's playing the severe mistress that doesn't grant me anything unless I work for it really, really hard. For the rest of the time, I wear a cock cage."

"Do you want that?"

"Oh, yes! I want it that way. She's got power over me. That's the thrill, and I wanna feel it. See, other people thrive on white water rafting, riding in a balloon, or jumping out of a plane with a parachute. I thrive on pain, on restrictions, on the feeling of being dominated to the max. That's the kick in my life. Not making money. I want . . ." He let the sentence trail off and looked toward the porch where the women were talking with each other. Lesley was gesturing with her hands. A moment later, they both laughed. "She's a great woman. Good looking, funny, an excellent business leader, and a good boss. She's clever, and she knows things about men." He lowered his chin.

"But she isn't looking for a relationship," Nick said quietly and resumed working.

"That's not yet decided. I wonder if I can convince her. I'm a patient man." Raiden smiled, but without joy. "I'm twenty-five. I don't have to tie the knot tomorrow."

Nicolas hid his thoughts behind a poker face. "Lesley's thirty-eight, just like Jacky. If women at that age haven't thought about a lasting relationship, I think they won't. It's not their concept, doesn't fit their expectations of life."

Raiden let go of his breath. His good mood slipped away with it. "You think I'm fighting a lost cause here?"

"If marriage and children are your goals in life, you'd have to choose another woman, yes. But that's not it, right?"

Raiden leaned against the counter, his gaze resting on his mistress's back. "I want her — for more than a few hours in the dungeon. I love her dominance, her presence in my life, but I like everything about her. The way she is. The sensitive woman behind the leather. But — " He wet his lips as his gaze flicked to Nicolas. "She's hesitant to make the next step. There's that light in her eyes—she's trying to open up and then, as if she's afraid of her courage, she pushes me away again. And that's happened a few times during the last several weeks. It was an astonishing development." He smoothed his beard and pushed back his hair. "I try to understand her, to find a way to let her know that I wouldn't misuse her once she embraces me without the shackles that tie my hands and feet. You know, she places hungry kisses all over my body. I hear her breathing, and I know that she wants me as much as I want her. Yes, that's more than a dominatrix does in her dungeon, but she only does these things when I'm tied up. After that she's like a friend from the neighborhood."

"Do you know anything about her? More than you see?"

"No." He brought the empty breadbasket in from the dining room. "I hoped that when I stayed a long time at the dungeon, she'd use the time for a chat, but if I ask, she smiles and dodges the question or counters with another. She knows quite a lot about me, but I'm not the one clamming up."

Nicolas didn't want to burst his bubble of hope. All that he knew about Lesley was based on stories Jacklyn had told him. He would not violate her faith in his confidentiality. "She's a woman who needs a long time to gain trust. Maybe you have to be patient."

"That won't change." He took the glass of water Nicolas offered. "Until then, I'll enjoy the chastity device around my jewels and she's got the key."

When Thomas was allowed to leave the black box, he squinted into the light that fell through the glass and steel ceiling. As he had expected, he was imprisoned in a factory building, large and airy and at least a hundred years old. While the former owners had left it to rot — there were still signs of decay in a few corners — the new one had renovated the building and inserted innovations no one had dreamed of during the last century. The cells were made of steel bars, if not completely of steel like the black box he had left. He noticed surveillance cameras every fifty feet and locked doors between the blocks, just like in any prison. The new owner had also installed a fight ring in the center of the first floor, visible to everyone from the upper corridors.

Handcuffed and escorted by two guards with angry faces, Thomas was taken to a shower room, where he had to drop his clothes. Standing in the tepid water, Thomas scrutinized his captors. One of them seemed to be from South America — tanned, black-haired, built like a martial arts fighter, with strong forearms and a thick neck. He smoothed his goatee from time to time. It seemed to be a nervous habit. The second man appeared to be of American origin — short-cropped light brown hair, crew cut, stocky like a wrestler. Both looked like no-nonsense prison wardens who held themselves back but would break bones if they had to. Thomas didn't buy the artificial aggressiveness, though. The men were under orders and wouldn't maim a prisoner unless forced.

Thomas enjoyed washing sweat and dirt off his body but feared what he had to face afterward. *A lot can happen in the middle of nowhere.*

He hadn't seen an exit. Even if he wrestled the two guards, he wouldn't know where to go. He didn't how many men were on shift in the building and how the estate was secured. He couldn't tell the strength of the fences, if there were any. He wondered how such an old building had been remodeled without anyone asking questions. He couldn't tell which states they had crossed and where he was being kept, only that the ride had taken all night.

The question of why he'd been kidnapped was still unanswered. Did someone want ransom or information? Was he a part of a much greater criminal activity, and he would meet with colleagues who were working the same case? Thomas looked up to find a third guard filming him with his cell phone. From one moment to the next, Thomas's hope that this was a kidnapping for reasons he could fathom vanished to be replaced by a profound fear that he was being kept to fulfill a crazy man's sexual desire. He was sick to his stomach and had to lean against the wall while the water poured down his body.

"Turn around!"

Thomas hesitated, breathing deeply, trying to regain his composure. He stood with his head bowed until the order was repeated and the two guards came closer. Though it galled him, he didn't find a reason to fight over such a matter.

The guard with the cell phone moved closer, catching his body from top to bottom.

"What's this about? Why are you doing this?" He didn't get an answer. Frustrated, he turned off the water. "Who's paying you?"

The South American threw him a towel, a pair of boxer shorts, and a t-shirt. "Get dressed!"

Every move Thomas made was recorded. He dropped the towel and put on the clothes quickly.

"Kneel!"

"What for?" Thomas retreated. The third guard was satisfied, nodded toward the others and left. "What do you want from me?"

Both guards pulled bats out of their belts and moved closer. Thomas loathed giving in. He longed to fight, but common sense told him he had no chance to win and would risk injuries that would keep him from escaping at a more suitable moment. Judging by the security measures, a team of armed men was downstairs to catch him once he set foot in the yard.

He knelt.

The second guard put a collar around his neck and locked it. "If you try to speak now, it'll hurt."

Thomas lowered his chin and closed his eyes. The situation was getting worse by the minute. His hands were cuffed behind his back while the third guard returned with hair clippers and an electric razor. Within ten minutes, Thomas had a buzz cut and his three-day stubble was gone.

"All right, that's enough. Up! You go back in lockup."

Lesley unlocked the door to her *Cave of Love* and offered Jacklyn and Nicolas the chance to choose a room they wanted. Since Nicolas had no say in this matter, Jacklyn walked straight toward the Medieval Torture room. Lesley followed, with Raiden right behind her.

Nicolas had seen the interior once and without interest. Now he became aware of the dedication to detail—the St. Andrew's cross, the rack, the pillory. The rough stone walls were hung with chains, whips, and ancient looking shackles side-by-side with flags and armorial bearings. His gaze was caught on a large Iron Maiden that hung from the rearmost wall.

"Yes, we feature an Iron Maiden," Lesley confirmed. "But it's for show. Though I admit I had a customer eager to try it."

"What did you do?" Nicolas asked, amused.

Lesley laughed. "I pretended it didn't work."

"And he believed you?"

She lowered her chin and her voice. "I distracted him with the wooden horse over there. It's no less cruel, but without nails that puncture your skin and kill you slowly."

"One of the dungeon rules, huh? Better not kill the customer."

Lesley bent over to whisper confidentially, "The first rule of the dungeon—nobody talks about the dungeon." She straightened, grinning. "Joking apart, the customer and I sign a contract. He agrees to my treatment—outlined by his wishes—and I take care that he isn't physically harmed beyond any named agreement. I observe my customers and I deny them treatments which they wouldn't withstand. That's the main rule for all my girls. No matter the customer's eagerness, the mistress decides what a customer can stomach. I fired a girl who whipped a customer too hard. Yes, he said he wanted it, but I don't." She shook her head, and all amusement had gone from her eyes. Now she was the businesswoman with respect and circumspection. She had a keen understanding of what her customers wanted. Her business flourished and had a good reputation because the customers knew they were safe. "If a customer's dissatisfied with the service, he's free to call it a day and leave. I know there are some crazy crackpots out there who wouldn't mind broken bones, but if they want that, I send them away. They can ask a guy on drugs for a mutual combat and have it their way."

"You know that mutual combat is illegal?"

"I know it is here." Lesley rolled her eyes. "You can't convince guys that some beatings are too harsh for them. If you tell them that they'd faint, they're angry because they think they can stomach it. I've seen it all."

"Me, too." Jacklyn pulled Nicolas by the sleeve. "You really need to lose your clothes." She turned to Lesley and Raiden. "And you get lost. I want my sub for me. Out."

Nicolas didn't need to look back to know that both Lesley and Raiden were disappointed.

Long before Jacklyn had worked at a dungeon, she had read about medieval torture devices, both disgusted at and thrilled by the machines men had built to force criminals, as wells as innocents, to confess.

The rack in the theme room of the Middle Ages was eight

21

feet long and four feet wide, made of thick wood to accommodate the strongest man. Manacles for hands and feet, connected by chains to a wheel under the rack's center, were meant to keep the prisoner in position and stretch his limbs until the muscles and sinews would rip apart. The ligaments would follow so that the prisoner would die a horribly slow death. It was one of the most vicious torture instruments of the dark age.

"You're impressed by the contents of the medieval room, huh?" Jacklyn twirled the crop in her hand. She bent toward her bound lover and let him look into her décolleté. One move too many and her boobs would fall out of the complicated construction of leather and lace. It was a fancy corselet but terribly hard to put on. "Or are you more impressed with my outfit?"

Nicolas wiggled his hands and toes. "I'm tied up on a rack. I won't say a wrong word or you'll tighten the chains once again. It's pretty intense."

"And it's just the beginning." She caressed his chest and abs with the crop, satisfied when she drew goosebumps. Due to the stress she'd put him in, Nicolas's veins stood out prominently. She traced every one of them, shivering with lust. "I shouldn't say it, but you, tied like this—you're a turn on for every woman."

Nicolas groaned.

Giggling, Jacklyn lowered her head to caress his nipples with her tongue, keeping eye contact with her lover, and relishing the love she saw in his eyes. She couldn't think of a better way to spend a day. "You want more, don't you?"

"Do you want my arms to be as long as my legs?"

"Aw, that won't happen." She turned her attention to his crotch, first with her fingernails, then when Nicolas held his breath, she used the crop from his abs down to his thighs. She was gentle around his genitals, but hit his abs and legs harder every time, until red welts showed. "You can take much more, my beautiful Beast." She paused to stand between his legs and devoted her attention to his growing erection. The Wartenberg wheel rolled along his inner thighs, and after a pause to make her sub understand what was about to happen, across his scrotum and penis.

Nicolas panted. His legs twitched as he tried in vain to move away from the stings. Jacklyn was aroused by his expression — the mix of discomfort and growing arousal that would soon wipe out the pain and make him ask for more. She let the wheel glide over his soles, knowing the pain was exquisite and stimulating for the submissive. As she had expected, Nicolas gasped and lifted his head.

"What is this? What're you doing to me?"

"Be quiet!" she warned and picked up the crop again. "Or you'll regret it."

With a smile, Nicolas surrendered to his destiny.

"That's better." Jacklyn whipped him leisurely, without much impact and only to get him into the mood.

After more than three years of partnership with benefits, Jacklyn knew about Nicolas's preferences. Cautiously, she explored his limits every time they played and was astonished at how far she was allowed to go. In the beginning, she had informed him about every step. She had taught him the moves and how tying him up intensified her emotions and would lead him to outstanding orgasms. She had restricted him with ropes or shackles but had not hurt him. The more he trusted her, the more she introduced him to bondage games that involved sex combined with pain. Visits to her best friend's dungeon were the latest addition and more entertaining than she had thought. He had surprised her by accepting her proposal for an hour at the *Cave of Love*, but then Nicolas was always good for a surprise. She loved that he was willing to explore new territory and follow her lead. Jacklyn hadn't had a lover in her life who had been a straight man without any contact to the wonderful world of bondage. Nicolas considered himself her apprentice, and she was a teacher with endless patience, knowing that he needed time to adjust to her ideas. She rewarded him generously for his growing cooperation, so that they both had a fulfilled love life.

She changed the crop for large nipple clamps and felt the surge of arousal when Nicolas hissed upon her fastening them. At the same time, his breathing accelerated, a definite sign that his expectations were rising. Jacklyn grinned as she strutted back toward his hips and put on her velvet gloves. After the beating came the massage of his cock and balls, one of the special treats reserved for her lover. Giving a man what he needed to get aroused was another of her specialties. The years as a mistress in Philadelphia served her well — she knew a lot about the male physique and how men could be stimulated. There was no doubt that Jacklyn served Nicolas well. His sex drive was one of a kind. It was a fact that he grudgingly — and to her amusement — allocated to her treatment. He admitted that his interest in sexual intercourse had increased with every month that he knew her.

She treated his shaft with care, knowing how to make him horny. It was her privilege that Nicolas reacted to her stimulation — and her stimulation only. She would scratch another woman's eyes out if she got wind of her having interest in her lover. His participation in the resulting short quarrel wouldn't be required.

When Nicolas was on the verge of orgasm, Jacklyn stopped, satisfied to have him driven this far. In the beginning, he had begged her, but now he knew better.

"You learned a lot," she teased, then took off the gloves and straddled his chest. Leisurely, she ran her fingernails through his freshly cut hair. When she kissed him, she let her tongue glide along his gums, the fastest way to make him yearn for more. Jacklyn looked into his eyes. She had trouble following her plan and making him wait. She wanted his climax. She wanted to see his face at the moment of orgasm, when pain and the heat of sex became one. Though they played the game frequently, she never got tired of his reaction in the moment of highest arousal.

His look spoke of love and devotion and that he cherished his partner as much as she cherished him. Jacklyn kissed his lips, his chin, his chest. Slowly, she inched along his body.

Jacklyn was far more flexible than any woman Nicolas had had sex with before, and she was wearing high-heeled boots, as if to increase the difficulty of sitting across his lap. She teased his cock by lowering her body onto his. Teasing. Just a small, brief contact. Teasing. Nicolas couldn't lift his hips to meet her halfway, and clenching his butt cheeks didn't help. The minutes he spent on the rack had taken their toll. His arms and legs hurt and were going numb. Jacklyn touched his glans with her wetness, let him enter an inch only to move away again, granting him nothing.

"You're playing it tough, ma Belle."

Jacklyn frowned but bent down to ease the strain on his limbs. Casually, she took away the clamps and licked his nipples. Once more, Nicolas was torn between pain and the overwhelming arousal that came with her gentle touch. He felt as if every nerve in his body stood on end. His breathing was shallow. He couldn't wait for her next move.

"You taste so sweet," she cooed. "I might take a bite of you."

Nicolas panted and felt his heart ram against his ribcage while Jacklyn licked his chest, his abs, and then—as if she'd stumbled over it—enclosed his member with her lips. Nicolas wanted to bow his back, but had no room. He flexed his toes, clenched and unclenched his fists, and wished for his lover to make him come, no matter how. Her teeth scraped along his length, up and down in a steady rhythm, but when he was convinced she'd bring him over the top, she stopped again.

"Fuck!"

"No bad language." Jacklyn used her nails again along his body. "If you don't hold your temper, I might leave you here."

"As my mistress commands."

"That's much better." Jacklyn kissed him again as if to drink him down.

He enjoyed the stimulation but wanted more. Being left on the brink of orgasm more than once had never been on his wish list. No other lover had demanded of him to hold back, to wait, to react on command only. Jacklyn's approach—teasing mixed with punishment—had changed his behavior. He experienced his orgasms more consciously, more clearly. The impact was often so intense his blood pressure dropped afterward, and he lost a moment in time. For the life of him, he wouldn't want another way of lovemaking ever again, even if his numb limbs spoke another language.

Jacklyn took her place across his lap again. Nicolas held his breath. His mistress dictated the rhythm. She took her time. She did what she wanted, and only when she reached her climax was he allowed to follow.

The Player waddled through the musty smelling corridor and casually looked at his short-fingered hands. He needed a manicure and checked his cell phone to find a free day for an appointment. The lovely Korean beautician was one of his favorite guests at his loft, but he was far away from that right now. Sighing, he conceded he wouldn't be home for another week. The manicure as well as the massage had to wait. There were important matters he had to attend. Neither of them allowed any delay.

The Player had a fine sense for new business opportunities. Unlike other criminals, who kept a façade of righteousness, the Player used front men for deliveries, arrangements, and to put pressure on unruly partners. The Player preferred to show his face to only a few people. Almost bald and slightly overweight with deep scars from an accident in his youth that not even plastic surgery could remove, he knew he was no easy man to look upon. From experience, he knew he had no chance to charm a woman, no matter his good manners. He despised that the so-called normal people turned their heads away from him or — if they were better behaved — cloaked their rejection with a false smile. He had suffered so many uncomfortable, painful and even cruel treatments by others in his youth and adolescence, he now avoided contact with the outer world. His partners in crime accepted him without aversion, for he was intelligent and sly. It was in his eyes — he didn't need a weapon to intimidate partners as well as customers. If he wished, he used his glare to keep opponents at bay. His men would come in later should verbal intimidation fail. In his twenty years of business, he had eliminated a number of enemies, in several cases to avoid competition, in other cases because he preferred to be rid of someone who might turn into an enemy in the end.

The Player considered his reclusive lifestyle his best defense, and yet he was unwilling to live like a hermit. He loved sex in many varieties, including willing women and men. During the last two years, he had developed a preference for strong guys — men with muscles in the right places. Consequentially, he created a new venture that included young studs who knew how to fight. He delighted in seeing them crash their fists against each other and struggle to stay conscious knowing that the loser might never return to his cell. The Player was astonished at how fast his business was growing—the wealthy gamblers with more money than they'd ever spend in their lifetime came to him, eager to bet, eager to watch a fight at the ring. The more blood was spilled, the better for the bets and the level of entertainment. A part of his mind resented the bloodlust others displayed, in spite of his own criminal intention and his ruthlessness. The other part counted the money he made which financed his extraordinary lifestyle. He had built a secretive empire with more influence than the great American corporations had in the last ten years.

Using his connections to local politicians, the Player bought an old industrial area with decaying buildings and enough surrounding open space to keep rubbernecks at a distance. Within five months, he had the buildings remodeled with barred cells, training rooms, and a fighting arena.

In another building, further to the south on the estate, he installed special entrances for the audience so that they wouldn't meet with the fighters at the prison. The building resembled an old boxing arena, but it was much better secured. He didn't want the fighters to escape and thus destroy his profit.

The auctions held in tandem were beginning to yield a profit. Customers were skeptical whether they could copy the Player's business model to their locations, but during the first auction three months earlier, five men who looked like cover models had changed owners for a large sum of money and the agreement that the men would never be set free again. The customers had happily claimed that they'd use their toys as long as they pleased and let them disappear afterward. By signing the contract, the customers accepted that they were bound for a harsh punishment if they didn't fulfill their obligations. The Player's reputation was well known from other business areas, so nobody doubted that he would execute his threats.

Looking down into the boxing ring, enclosed by a steel cage so that the fighters couldn't leave without permission, the Player was satisfied. He was a mastermind of modern business and a rich man, on top of that.

He walked toward the rows of cells to have a look at his latest acquisition, a man from Washington, DC, kidnapped on request of one of his Mexican partners and his associate from Virginia, who behaved like a hungry hyena with an equally unpleasant laugh. The Player was curious about the reasons why the man had been selected and yet hadn't asked. The sensation of unknown circumstances was like spice on a good slice of meat.

He looked through the bars into the cell. "He was brought here recently?"

"Yes, sir," Kevin answered, half a step behind him. He was one of the trustworthy assistants the Player employed.

"Did he eat, drink?" He glanced over his shoulder. "Does he have a name?"

"He did. Thomas Zutarski."

The Player nodded curtly, content with his employee's answer. Kevin wasn't a loquacious person but was competent and respectful, two character traits that he cherished more than eloquent speech.

The fighter sat on the mattress and looked up with hate-filled eyes. He didn't say a word, and that was for a reason. The Player preferred the fighters to be restricted by a shock collar that caused severe pain if the man tried to speak. That way, the Player could scrutinize his latest acquisition without being bothered by shouts and complaints. He was never in the mood to answer questions concerning why and by whom the man was kidnapped. It was usually enough to gag the men during the first days of captivity. The longer they stayed in the cells, the fewer questions they asked, but he allowed the prisoners to talk with each other. He wasn't that cruel.

Thomas had wide shoulders, strong arms, and muscled legs. His eyes spoke of intelligence and his bearing told of a man used to enduring difficult situations without panicking. Though he'd been in the dark room for eight hours without contact with anyone, he was neither shaking with fear nor running around agitated like a caged animal. The Player was impressed and curious.

"Any problems with the kidnapping?"

"None." Kevin clasped his hands in front of his body, lifted his clean-shaven chin, and waited patiently.

"News from the police concerning his disappearance?"

"Yes. He's been declared a kidnapped person. The local police handed the case to the FBI."

The Player's brows twitched. "That was fast."

"He works for the ATF."

The Player suppressed any indication of his surprise at the last moment, but turned and walked away from the cell. The news was most unwelcome. As it was his business priority, the Player had asked his Mexican partners whether the kidnapping would stir unrest anywhere. He had been assured that the victim's pregnant wife was a shy woman and therefore no threat. The man with the laughter of a hyena had even claimed that the woman would collapse and be unable to make a single decision. In the light of the man's profession, the Player expected the ATF in collaboration with the FBI would investigate more thoroughly than the local police would've done. He turned to Kevin, who followed him a step behind.

"Find out what the FBI knows."

"Will do."

"And I want to know why they wanted him kidnapped so badly. I don't like to be kept in the dark like this."

"Yes, sir."

Kevin turned away and left the Player pondering his next move. He walked back toward the cell to scrutinize the prisoner once more. Judging by his appearance, the ATF employee had fighting skills and therefore potential. If he lost, he could serve another purpose. The Player switched on his cell phone to make a call while he walked toward his office.

Thomas listened to the sounds around him. Downstairs, there were two men fighting and a third one barking commands about how to corner the opponent. *Illegal fights? Can it be that easy?*

The strange scarred man had gone, leaving Thomas guessing the reason for his kidnapping. The way he'd been scrutinized, Thomas hoped that the video was meant to inform someone about his looks and strength, not how well he was equipped. The cell to his left was empty. In the cell to his right, a dark-skinned man was sleeping on the cot. His face bore signs of a fight, and his knuckles were bloody. In the cell after the next one, a tall, blond man leaned against the bars, hanging his head, sighing deeply. His face and arms looked like a landscape of red and dark purple bruises, including a black eye. Like Thomas, the man's hair was cut very short, and he wore nothing but boxer shorts and a muscle shirt.

A fight club. What a bad joke! But why me?

If he wasn't mistaken, the men he saw were in their twenties and in great shape. Thomas had turned thirty-two a month ago. Though he was fit, he wouldn't beat a young and experienced fighter. His days of regular martial arts training lay behind him. Frustrated to be stuck without answers and without the chance to ask questions, Thomas stood and drank water. His stomach rumbled.

To distract himself from his misery, Thomas thought about Charlene.

He pictured her round, juvenile face, her blonde hair, now cut to a fashionable bob. He imagined her smile that he saw every time he came home. She welcomed him with a heart-warming embrace and held him tight as if she'd never let him go again. Because of her dreadful childhood and the events at Florence Town, Charlene had become distrustful of people, but not of him. He loved a sensitive woman who rewarded him with unlimited devotion. She would go with him every-where, without question. After their reunion and his recovery from a bullet wound, they had spent a few days at the beach, and close to him, she had dared to swim in the ocean. They had made love at the small motel and enjoyed every minute. She was the woman of his dreams, not an arrogant woman with high expectations like his first wife, but a warm and en-chanting soul. Charlene loved Thomas for his heart. He'd never felt better in his entire life.

To stay away from dangerous jobs, he had decided to leave the ATF after his undercover mission, but his boss, Vernon Freeman, convinced him to accept an office position instead so that the bureau wouldn't lose an intelligent and resourceful agent. The money was good and financed the little house they had bought. Charlene had whooped with joy that they owned a place to stay and that Thomas would be home more often. He still recalled her exuberance the day he'd shown her his revised contract with the bureau. During his first week at the office, she had told him of her pregnancy.

He had hoped that from that day on his life would be nor-mal, wonderful. They would start a family and enjoy the hap-piness of parenthood.

In the next cell, the dark-skinned man stirred and turned to look at him.

"If I didn't know better, I'd bet your mistress lets you have a hell of a time." Nicolas offered Raiden a place at the small round table in the bar next to the dungeon. A waitress served two beers and a bowl with mixed nuts and another with nachos and a dip. The nocturnal entertainment hadn't yet started, so they had Lesley's bar to themselves.

Raiden swung his butt onto a bar stool, grinning all over his bearded face. "How would you know? Aren't you the poor soul who's always left without satisfaction?"

They toasted with the beer mugs.

"Where're the ladies?"

"You know what's said about snakes—they need time to shed their skin."

"Ouch." Nicolas made a face, laughing. "The clothes they wear are tight enough, that's true. I could fetch my buzz saw. That would make quick work of them."

"And cut the ropes? Hey, that's a heavy machine for ropes."

"Ropes?" Nicolas shook his head in mock dismay. "Man, you don't know anything about the wonderful world of appliquéd lace, furbelow, and plicated selvage."

"But I know how to undress a lady without cutting off her skin."

"If you ever had your hands free, you might even do it." Nicolas craned his neck to see the entrance. "Should we go and offer help? Maybe they put a lot of knots into those fancy loops and can't get out."

"Yeah, let's help them. I'm a master of knots."

"I'd like to peel my lady out of the boots. They look like they're glued on."

"If it's glue, you'll need more than your fingers."

"Oh, I'd know where to put my fingers."

Raiden laughed out loud and slapped the table so hard that

the waitress lifted her gaze. "Yeah, I bet you do!" He drank and put down his mug with a satisfied sigh. "Ah, isn't that a wonderful day? Breakfast and a session. How was yours?"

"I should check if I'm Mr. Fantastic." Nicolas looked at his maltreated wrists. His ankles looked the same, and Jacklyn had apologized, at least a little bit.

"The rack, huh? I've got good memories of that one."

"It was great, the moment feeling returned to my limbs."

Staring at his mug, Raiden's voice was dreamlike. "You grant her power over you. Though you strive for satisfaction, you know that she's close to an orgasm seeing you struggle in your shackles. She loves how you fight, and she loves how you endure the pain." He grinned, drank beer, and wiped his lips.

"No doubt. I'm happy when she's happy."

Raiden furrowed his brows.

Nicolas admitted that Lesley's description of her pet being a lion was accurate. The marks of a tight collar and abrasions from manacles around his wrists only added to the animalistic appearance. Furthermore, his skin color and the amber eyes turned him into an exotic specimen, able to turn the women's heads. Nicolas wondered whether his team members and friends knew of his sexual preferences and how they dealt with them.

Raiden reached under his shirt, grimacing.

"The nipple rings?" Nicolas made a face. "Your idea?"

Raiden dropped his hand. "Itchy. Yeah, the rings were my idea, four years ago when I was on a heavy pain trip." He smacked his lips. "I was crazy enough to tell the lady I wouldn't want any local anesthetic. Stupid, right? She said she'd do it but at my risk. I could stand the first ring and fainted when it was done. The lady told me she wouldn't do that shit again and sent me away." Raiden laughed, loud and heartily. "But I needed to know what I could stomach, I really did. The second one was done the usual way. Much better."

"And it had to be rings?"

"Yup. You can't fasten chains to barbells. I thought it was a fucking great idea for bondage, but the professionals don't touch them."

"Because of the risk of physical harm."

"Exactly. *Play it safe, play it sane.* At that time, I didn't want to hear about safety reasons or anything like that. I was twenty-one. Now I know better. But it took me a while to convince my mistress to use them as she pleases." His look was warm and knowing. "I didn't intend to shock you."

"I'm an FBI agent. You need more than nipple rings to shock me."

"I bet. But tell me — if Jacky broke up with you — would you miss being tied up?"

Nicolas flinched. "Two years ago, I'd have denied that. Now it's a clear *yes.*" He looked away from Raiden, who appeared to analyze his feelings better than any doctor of psychology ever would. "To be honest — she trained me. She awoke a desire within me that I hadn't expected. She taught me how much I'd missed so far. Now that I know how good an orgasm can be, I don't know whether I could go without. I would urge my lover to tie me up and cause me pain." The confession sounded strange in his ears, but it was still true.

"You thrive on a strong emotion. Oh, I know how that feels." Raiden hummed with contentment. "How was it for you the first time?"

Involuntarily, Nicolas laughed. "The first time I was very skeptical. When Jacky mentioned ropes, I didn't have the faintest idea what I was in for. She tied my hands, and I asked myself whether I was ready to trust her and give up my freedom." He ate a handful of nuts. "I wasn't."

"What did she do?"

"She stopped, put away the ropes, and cuddled with me."

He nodded slowly. "It's all about trust. Nothing else matters."

Raiden emptied his beer mug and wrinkled up his nose. "In a dungeon it's much easier. You come, you choose a mistress or a master, and you make an arrangement. No matter how hard you want it, you know you'll be free once the time's up."

"Did you try to find a woman who . . . would fulfill your wishes and more?"

Raiden leaned back, sighing. "Not until I met Lesley. I couldn't stand a normal woman with normal desires." He laughed and slapped the table. "I don't even know if I'm able to get a boner without feeling pain!"

Nicolas didn't mention that a love life made you horny in a way no tethers could. It seemed that Raiden had no experience of a girl who was devoted to him. He was in love with Lesley, who was as aloof as a Roman goddess. Nicolas pitied the young man, but got away without an answer because the ladies appeared.

"What took you so long?" Raiden asked, wiggling his brows and looking at Nicolas. "Knots?"

"Indeed." Jacklyn sighed. "Those damn corselets consist of longer ribbons than a fisherman's net!"

Raiden and Nicolas collapsed laughing and were unwilling to reveal the reason.

CHAPTER THREE

In the evening, a guard ordered Thomas to stand at the bars, then took off his shock collar with the distinct warning to keep his voice low.

"If you shout, insult the guards, or do anything we don't tolerate, the collar's back on and won't come off. Got it?" The guard didn't wait for an answer but left the collar on the other side of the corridor, clearly visible.

Thomas massaged his abused neck and took a deep breath.

The man in the next cell hung his forearms across the bars, grinning as if he'd met an old friend. "You must've impressed the bastards. I wore my collar for two days. And this *it doesn't come off again* is just for show. No one runs around with this thing all the time. They need it for the other freshmen." He gestured toward his chest. "Miguel. And you are?"

"Thomas. Call me Tom."

"All right, Tom. You're new here. Did you spend time in the black hole?"

"That's what you call it?"

"No one talks about anything here." Miguel had a distinct Spanish accent. "Either you call the things what you want or you have no words."

Thomas leaned against the opposite bars. "How long have you been here?"

"Three fight nights." He made a dismissive gesture. "Maybe three months or four? I lost count."

"Where were you kidnapped?"

"I wasn't." Miguel frowned, clearly surprised. "I learned of

37

a gang of smugglers in Tijuana. They're always looking for fighters. The offer was good." He pointed at his chest. "I'm the best fighter of my village. I won a lot of fights. I didn't know, though, that I'd end in a cell like this." He shrugged and made the sign of the cross. "My family's safe, and that's all that counts."

"Your family?" Thomas digested the information that obviously not everyone he saw was a kidnapping victim.

"They were taken to California, and I volunteered as a fighter, or *gladiator* as they call it. That was the price I had to pay."

"Do you know where we are? Which town?"

"No fucking idea. There are no landmarks I recognize."

"And the man with the scars? He's the boss?"

"Yes." Miguel looked at the corridor as if expecting a guard to come and forbid the conversation. When there were no sounds of approaching boots, he went on. "But he isn't much around. He's got helpers, lots of them." He sighed. "Someone will take care of my family so that they live a happy life in California. They said they've got friends there who'd take them in. That's all that counts."

Thomas opened his mouth to point out that no guarantee existed that his family wouldn't be exploited like him, but he had no reason to fire up Miguel's doubts. The fighter would win eventually, three fights or even four. However, there would be a time when he was too tired or too injured to fight. Thomas didn't want to think about the men who were no longer of use to the scarred gangster.

"What's the reason behind these fights?"

"Money. Bets. But there's much more." Miguel finger-combed his short black hair and made a face. "You should know — this is like a market . . . a bazaar. People come here to see you fight. Many people. Like a rock concert. Right. But that's only one part of what's going on here. I heard that if

38

certain people are interested in you, there's a chance that they buy you."

"*Buy me?*" Thomas choked on the words. "You mean this is a slave market? Human trafficking? For forced labor or worse? Are you serious?"

Miguel didn't understand the rush of words, so Thomas repeated his question more slowly. The prisoner nodded.

"Yes. A marketplace for men." He shrugged. "Some women, too, so I heard, but we don't see them. So it might be a rumor."

Thomas's heart pounded so fast it hurt. He tried to think, but the thoughts overtook each other, all of them demanding attention. "How many men are held prisoner here?"

Miguel shrugged. His haggard face was bare of pity. "Twenty, maybe thirty. The numbers change. Men come, men leave. I see them at the fights, but only a few while I'm here." He pointed toward the rows of cells on the other side of the corridor. "It's not like we meet in a cantina for a chat."

Thomas was sweating and his chest seemed too constricted to breathe. He understood the concept of illegal fights and the high sums of money people bet on the fighters. For decades, gangs had made money based on this concept. In most cases, the participants did it willingly to get their share of the profit. Those men returned home after the fights, and if they'd had enough, they left town. The scarred man had taken the business to another level. *Losing all hope is freedom.*

"Hey, Tom, are you okay? How did you come here?"

Thomas slipped down to sit on the narrow cot. He buried his face in his hands. "I was ripped away from my loved one, and I have no idea why I'm here."

"You promised you wouldn't answer the phone on your days off," Jacklyn said, glaring at Nicolas when he pulled the phone out of his jacket pocket. "Why can't you stick to the rule?"

"It's Vernon. He tried to reach me three times. He wouldn't call on a Sunday if it weren't important." He pressed the redial button. Vernon picked up after the first ring. "Hey, it's Nick. What's going on?"

"Sit down in case you're standing."

"All right." Frowning, Nicolas chose the couch. Jacklyn sensed his uneasiness and took the place beside him. "I'm sitting."

"Last night, Tom was kidnapped by six men with army training. They took him away in a new gray van. Teresa watched them leave but didn't catch the numbers on the plate. There has been no call since, so we don't know who took him or where he's being kept."

Nicolas flinched as if he had been punched in the stomach. "Did you call the FBI?"

"Of course. The hostage rescue team arrived a few hours later, put up their gear, and now we're waiting for a call from the kidnappers."

"What about Charlene?"

"She had a breakdown when she learned what happened. The doc gave her something to sleep. She's with us, of course. She stays here until Tom's back."

"I'm so sorry, Vernon. What did the CSU tell you?"

Vernon sighed. "They said the break-in was done professionally—both the front and back door were smashed with rams. The men wore night vision goggles, rubber boots, large guns. Tom could neither reach for his weapon nor make a call. His phone was found on the kitchen counter. Your call was the last one on it." He cleared his throat. "It might be good news that there was no blood on the kitchen floor, so they took him without hurting him. They wanted him alive."

Nicolas wiped his face with his free hand, exhaling. "All

right. Nothing happens without a reason. He was kidnapped either for ransom or for information. If I had to guess, it would be information. You said the kidnapping was done in military fashion. That would hint at a paramilitary group acting against the state. What was he working on?"

"Though that's obvious, I wouldn't assign the motive to his work. Tom accepted a desk job, and he'd recently started listing details of different kinds of explosives new on the illegal market." Vernon sounded depressed. "As much as I want to—I don't see a reason behind this act. I hoped you might have insight. You met with him regularly."

"We talk about our loved ones, about work sometimes, but he never mentioned enemies or people who caused him trouble. Are there any old cases still unsolved—with professional gangsters still on the run?"

Vernon sighed, and Nicolas heard him sit down hard on a chair that creaked pitifully.

"You're talking about the Turners."

"As far as I know—"

"Three men are still on the loose, yes, but we thought they had left the country. The last thing I know is that the Virginia State Police has them on their wanted list. I'll contact them for information. If you hear anything or if anything comes to mind, please, give me a call."

"Will do." Nicolas lowered the phone while Jacklyn put an arm around his trembling shoulders. "This is bad news. Really bad news."

The Player received news that another target had been acquired at the parking lot of an erotic shop next to one of DC's BDSM clubs. He smirked and finished the call with the distinct order that the area shouldn't be targeted for at least a month to stay out of the local police focus.

The Player was careful never to poach in his own back yard. Fresh fighters came from the east coast, preferably. The big cities proffered anonymity, neighbors didn't know each other, and if a man vanished, the police were easily convinced he had left for another town. The experience after several kidnappings revealed that without friends or relatives, people vanished without being missed. The Player had found out soon enough that the *Murder Capital* Washington, DC, was an ideal playground with a long list of potential victims.

He was annoyed that his Mexican partners — obviously in league with their obnoxious sidekick — had cajoled him into kidnapping Thomas, an employee of a federal bureau. To his chagrin, the FBI had put Thomas on a priority list, which meant that a unit of investigators were working on the case. It was an unwelcome setback and a mistake the Player wouldn't repeat. If the Mexicans — Juan and his brother in crime, Arturo — had told him the truth beforehand, the Player would've politely but decisively declined their request. He was still at odds with the Mexicans' inscrutable relationship with their American friend or business partner. The young man appeared to be driven by some kind of drug. He talked a lot, mumbled to himself, and was as aggressive as a hungry cobra. The Player had alerted Kevin to watch the man's whereabouts and throw him out the instant he stirred unrest or even provoked a fight.

Problems put aside, the Player had spent a few hours of pure bliss with a man and a woman — both blindfolded and sufficiently obedient to his wishes. He had taken the man first and made him satisfy the whore with his tongue. Her moaning had spurred his arousal, and she had been willing to grant the Player her best performance after that. High on the kick of orgasm, the Player had tied up the man to whip him. While the captive was groaning, he told the whore to give him a blowjob he wouldn't forget.

It had been a memorable night, and he had slept like a baby.

The Player stopped at Thomas's cell, where the man sat on the cot, hanging his head, exhausted. He had watched this new fighter during his first sparring, no more than thirty minutes, but enough to decide that the agent was nimble and knew how to box. If his information was correct, Thomas was trained in kickboxing and Jiu jitsu.

The Player stepped close to the bars, lifting a notepad. "You will sign the contract, and after that you'll fight for me."

Thomas lifted his head. Behind the tiredness hostility showed. "And if I don't? I'm not your toy you can put where you want."

"I prefer to call you a *gladiator*, but *toy* seems equally fitting." The Player smirked and lowered his hand. He wished he had sent Kevin. The conversation bored him. "Do you remember where my men caught you? This means that we know where your wife lives. If you don't sign the contract, my men will find and kill her."

Baring his teeth, Thomas rushed toward the door and held tight to the bars. "Leave her out of this!" His voice boomed along the corridor.

The Player moved his head left and right, loosening his neck muscles after a long workday. He wanted to go back to his bedroom and take another man with him. He had installed a small pillory close to his bed so that he could see the restrained victim while he read a book or watched TV. His crotch ached, but he refrained from putting a hand to it. "I'm not interested in Charlene. I'm interested in you and your fighting skills." He sighed, annoyed. His lawyer had stressed that contracts were necessary to maintain the appearance of a legal business, and nothing was more important than being able to show a contract should the police storm the building. "Sign the contract, or your dead wife is the last thing you see."

"And then? Will you kill me, too?" Thomas rattled the bars forcefully but in vain. "Is that the plan?"

Obviously, the Player had hit the right nerve, but he had no patience. The display of aggression pleased the Player and stirred his arousal. He wanted to leave, badly. "You're no good to me dead. But if you don't want to . . . I won't make you. There're other tasks I can use you for." He simpered again, then walked away with measured steps. "I have my men waiting in DC." He checked his watch. "Let's see . . . if they catch her now, she'll be here with you tomorrow at noon."

"No!"

The Player blew out air through his lips and hung his head as he stopped. "Will you sign?" he asked, turning around, and walking back slowly.

Thomas hung his head. "You don't leave me much of a choice."

"There was no choice to begin with." He lifted the notepad and the small plastic stick that was attached to it. "Don't try to wrest it from me. The guards will be with you faster than you can do any mischief, all right? And the result would be the same—the death of your wife." Still, the Player felt a twinge of anxiety when Thomas reached through the bars. His hands and forearms were strong, and he could throttle the Player right that moment.

Thomas scribbled his name on the empty line. "Why? Why a contract? You kidnapped me!"

"That's your interpretation." The Player took a deep breath as he stepped away from the bars. He decided to assign one of his helpers the next time. A confrontation was much too stressful at his age. "I have a contract with you concerning mutual combat. If ever someone comes asking, you're legally engaging in fights, based on this contract. It also says that you came to me voluntarily to make money." He shrugged. "The accommodation isn't the best place in town, but it suffices your needs, doesn't it?"

Thomas gaped at him, then, as if the news hit him, he moved backward, shaking his head. "You think you can pull this off? Pretend that I'm a contracted fighter? And that I agreed on being locked up here?"

"There are several men like you." The Player made an all-encompassing gesture. "Don't think all these men were kidnapped. Many of them want to be here."

"Trust a few. Fear the rest." Thomas leaned against the rear wall. A bitter laugh escaped him. "So, it's a contract. I can terminate a contract."

"Yes, but only after two years. It was in the fine print."

"But if I—"

"You won't tell anyone about this institution. No one knows that you're here. No one's interested in finding you." When Thomas lowered his chin, the Player's anger increased. "My men didn't leave tangible clues. They were in and out of your house in less than five minutes. No one saw anything. You might expect the police are searching for you, but no matter what they try, they won't find out where you are."

He couldn't stand another exchange of useless words and walked away, ignoring Thomas's shouts that the FBI wouldn't stop searching for him. The Player decided he had worked enough for a day and went to the lower level where his nocturnal entertainment waited for him. His pants were painfully tight.

"You're an important man, then?" Miguel asked when the scarred man had left for good.

Thomas hung his head and closed his eyes. He was devastated, and though he expected Charlene to stay with Teresa and Vernon, he couldn't stop thinking that the gangster boss was right—it was easy to locate Charlene. If asked nicely, the neighbors would tell about the friendly couple next door. They would tell about the little lady and her pregnancy and the couple she stayed with when Tom was out of town. It was a small step to find out their name. He feared that if he didn't cooperate, Teresa and Vernon would be in danger, too.

"You made him angry." Miguel wiped his stubbly chin. "But now you see how it works. It's a contract. You fulfill the contract and then you leave."

Thomas knew he should keep his mouth shut. "Miguel, I don't know you, and I don't know if you're always this gullible, but let me tell you this—you won't withstand fighting for two years. There will be someone better than you. Someone will come and knock you out. You'll lose. What do you expect to happen?"

Miguel pointed across his shoulder, shrugging casually. "Others lost, too. They're taken here. There's a doc around after the fights. He treats our injuries on the spot." He bobbed his head. "And when we feel better, there's another fight night."

"And that's it. You're imprisoned and only let out to fight. Do you want to endure this for two years? And even if you survive by a miracle, do you expect the boss to let you go?"

Miguel's eyes widened and his jaw dropped. "You think he'll cheat me?"

Thomas wanted to shake sense into him. He was reminded of the many honorable citizens of Florence Town who couldn't believe that the three big families were involved in crimes. Many inhabitants had tried to stop the FBI from arresting the men because they considered them upstanding and innocent citizens, benefactors of the community. "If you're really such a good fighter, why should he let you go? Don't forget, you could talk about what happens here every day. You could tell the police about me and the others, who aren't willing contractors. Have you thought about that?"

Miguel scratched behind his ear, looking miserable. "I never talk much with the others. I don't ask, you know? It's better that we stay . . . enemies."

Thomas lowered his chin and lifted his brows. "Hmm, you introduced yourself to me."

"Yeah, I know. That guy on the other side is an asshole, and it's hard not to talk to anyone all day long."

"So, there's not much entertainment during the day?" Despite his despair, Thomas tried to smile, but all he could do was twitch the corners of his mouth. "No TV program for the prisoners, huh?"

"*Nada.* There are meals, sparring, shower, a few hours in the backyard, and if you're lucky, you can work in the fields."

"Fields? There are fields close by?"

"This here, this is huge. It's an area of five hundred acres, at least. You can't even see the fences, but I was told there are fences." He sighed. "Believe me, you want to work sooner than later. If you've got nothing to do, it's hard."

"I see. And who chooses the men for the field work?"

"The guards. They take only those men who have been here for weeks and don't cause trouble."

Thomas's hope sparked that he might have a chance to escape while being outdoors.

Miguel grinned, granting sight of two rows of teeth more yellow than white. "They'll watch you closely, Tom. This isn't a walk in the park, if you get my meaning. The men wear leg irons, and two prisoners are shackled together. No one runs."

At the mention of leg irons, Thomas felt an icy shiver running down his back. While on an undercover mission, the Turner family had accused him of helping Charlene escape. Consequently he'd been sentenced to hard work and shackled whenever he left his cell. He had suffered at the cruel hands of Jebediah and Tyrone Turner, who had mistreated him at every turn. Only the intervention of Nicolas Hayes had saved him from being killed by the cousins. Due to the intense investigation of the FBI and the ATF, many members of the Turner family, except Tyrone and two other relatives, had been arrested and convicted to long terms in prison.

"You look terrible," Miguel said without a sign of pity. "Forget about running away. I don't think it's possible."

Thomas gathered his wits. "Tell me, what happens at a fight night?"

Miguel took a deep breath, made a contented sigh, and beamed at him. "That I can tell you . . ."

When Nicolas entered the office at the FBI building, Jason got up, grinning broadly. He appeared to hover above ground supported by an air of exuberance, and Nicolas was reminded of a comic character, Mr. Magoo, even though Jason had more hair.

"Guess what I have to tell you!" Jason stood in front of his desk, and the joy in his words made Nicolas's heart ache.

"A good morning to you, partner. It looks like you had a fabulous weekend."

"Ah, yes!" Jason helped Nicolas out of the coat. "Elaine told me that—" He made a dramatic pause in which Nicolas turned around. "She's pregnant!"

Nicolas put his coat away and hugged his partner. "Wow! That's great news! I'm so happy for you!" He patted Jason's shoulders. "I hope everything works out for both of you."

"Sure. Sure it will." Jason let out a big breath and handed Nicolas his morning coffee. "And you? What happened in your life?"

Nicolas hated to ruin Jason's mood. "Well, we had a nice time and . . . then, there's bad news. Thomas was kidnapped."

"Your friend from the ATF? Oh, my god." Jason sat down,

his happiness blown away. "How? Why? Is the HRT on the case?"

"Armed men. We don't know the reason. Yes, HRT arrived, but so far, the kidnappers haven't called. Vernon and I think there could be a connection to the Turner case, but we have no proof."

"It's a start. If I remember it correctly, the Turners were in league with drug smugglers from Mexico, right? Could it be they're connected with the kidnapping? As a revenge for their blown-up operation? They lost a lot of money that day."

"If so, they'd have killed Thomas once they had a chance. It's unlikely they would go the long way and kidnap him. Where would they take him? And the Mexicans didn't leave the impression they had army personnel among them. Teresa said the men had military equipment and acted like a well-trained team. No, Jason, the Mexicans would've come and riddled the house with bullets."

"Will you volunteer to help with the investigation?"

Nicolas knew Jason wouldn't be able to stand his absence. "I thought about it, but Sullivan wouldn't sign a delegation paper. Not without good reason. And we have to do the paperwork for the last case."

Jason moaned. "I'd hoped Matt would do this, but he's on vacation." He switched on his computer. "Too suddenly, for my taste."

Nicolas's thoughts drifted to where Thomas might be kept. Remembering how Thomas had suffered while investigating in Florence Town, Nicolas hoped his friend would stay sane.

Thomas learned from Miguel that only fighters who were fit and able joined the fight night. A man named Kevin, the boss's right hand, selected the combatants. The fighters were taken by bus to another building, a twenty-minute ride from the prison. Close to the arena and visible to the audience, a large cage displayed the *gladiators* chosen to fight each other.

Grudgingly, Miguel admitted that his village fights had more regulations than he found here. Though the men looked alike, they had different experiences and qualifications. Several of them had learned how to box, another group knew karate while others used their massive bodies to ram their opponents against the fences. The fights lasted until the loser was unconscious or dead. Every style was tolerated, and the loser was thrown out while the promoter announced the winner and the results of the bets. Miguel couldn't tell whether every loser was taken back to his cell. Thomas assumed that the guards and the boss decided which fighter survived. The method explained why the numbers changed and men vanished. It was obvious that the boss needed fresh fighters on a regular basis, either by luring them with money or promises or by kidnapping those who didn't join voluntarily.

He shivered. "Tell me about the market."

"I can't. Not in detail, anyway." Miguel lifted and dropped his shoulders and hands in an exaggerated way. "Once, I saw a second group of men being led through a door and into another room. I suppose it's a kind of dining room. Big. It was well-lit and had a nice floor. The men taken there look different from us — the *gladiators*." He rubbed his chin and avoided eye contact. "Let's say, they're kind of . . . dandy. And they were heavily tethered."

Thomas lowered his chin and wiped his face with one hand, trying and failing to digest the range of cruelty the boss displayed. In his years of service, Thomas had heard of human trafficking and its many varieties. It seemed that the scarred boss had built up a complex enterprise. Once more, the question arose of how he could've done it under the noses of local police forces and other authorities responsible for the compounds in their county. Was it possible the boss and his men acted without being seen? How could they maintain a compound with water and electricity, supply the prisoners with food and clothes without someone from the next town noticing the unusual shopping list? *What's the pretense?*

"If they take the men there to show them—did you see guests go there, too?"

"Sure. After the fights." Miguel looked uneasy. "I don't know how to say this. There are the fights in the arena, and when the guests have had enough, they can go to that room."

"And have a look at the men for sale." Thomas ran a hand over his very short hair. "A slave market on US soil. *The impossible true story.* I feel like I've been hit in the guts."

"Better recover quickly. You're wanted for another sparring."

CHAPTER FOUR

If Thomas learned one thing from the hard sparring, it was that he was in better shape than he had expected. However, he was bone-tired when he finally returned to his cell. A plate with food and fresh water waited for him. He ate hungrily and didn't look up when Miguel made a sound of disgust. Only when a man stopped in front of his cell did Thomas lift his head.

He stopped breathing, and the spoon slipped from his hand.

In his mind, he had confronted and bashed Tyrone Turner a hundred times. Seeing him in black jeans and a dark blue leather jacket with a toothpick between his lips and the arrogant smile of a winner, Thomas wanted to crash through the bars and throttle his enemy until he was dead.

It was an effort to swallow the last bite and put down the plate. "What're you doing here, you scum?"

Tyrone leaned his lanky frame against the railing. He cocked his head and crossed his arms and his ankles, looking as satisfied as a cat with cream. He let the toothpick slip from one side to the other.

"Shouldn't the question be — *what am I doing here*?"

"Phrase it as you want — it's all the same. What stone did you crawl out from under?" Thomas got up, too restless to sit. His pulse was racing. His enemy was almost in reach, and his instinct urged him to kill him. He cursed that he was locked up when his hands wanted to be around his enemy's throat. "How did you escape the police?"

Tyrone grinned and waved away the question, shrugging. "Aren't you surprised to be here? I mean, you're not the type they want here. You're an old bone, fucker."

Thomas frowned, trying to put meaning to the young dude's words. "Then open up and let me go home."

"Home? You want to go *home*?" Out of the blue, Tyrone's oblong face contorted with anger, and his pretended equanimity was gone. The toothpick fell from his lips. "You took *my home* away from me. You know, I had it all — women, fun, good friends. Now I'm on the run with my Mexican friends, but I miss my life. I really do." He stepped closer to the bars, teeth bared like an aggressive animal. "But you understand me, don't you? You're away from your woman, too. Now you see what you've done to me."

"Done to you?"

"You deprived me of my home."

"Your home?" Thomas held tight to the bars as if to rip them off their hinges. "You committed crimes, you miserable shithead! You used the premises to deal with drugs!"

"Only to create a new income. Our grandfather ran the business into the ground. We had no choice."

"No choice? Three people were killed in town. Eight more died in the first bomb explosion!"

"Serving a greater good." Tyrone shrugged.

Thomas wished he could press his body through the bars. "*Some family secrets are best kept buried.*" He was sickened by Tyrone's displayed gullibility. "You killed people for profit!"

"I did what I had to do. It was necessary for the family." He grinned the sleazy grin of a hyena. "And you'd do anything for your family, too, huh?"

Thomas clung to the bars and closed his eyes, nauseated. He didn't see a way he could convince Tyrone of his wrongdoing. He wanted to smash the young man's face, but the fence between them was as impenetrable as Tyrone's foolishness. Thomas had never before felt so helpless.

"Oh, I see you want to hit me again, huh? The way you did in the stall." Tyrone pointed at Thomas. "I haven't forgotten how you bashed me and almost broke my wrist. But that's over. I'm the one calling the shots now. I'm the one who brought you here. And you'll bleed, man, oh yes, you'll bleed."

Thomas lifted his head. "What're you talking about?"

Tyrone laughed out loud. "You haven't heard? You'll fight for your life in three days."

"Fight for my life?"

"Oh, come on, don't be so blockheaded! Do you think you were hauled here to display your bare chest? There are guys who'll wipe the floor with your face. I chose them! If the first one doesn't kill you, the next one will."

Thomas wiped his mouth with his hand, too shocked for words. He had believed that the fight was over once a fighter went down and didn't get up again, just like in any boxing tournament. If Tyrone used his influence, Thomas wouldn't make it out of the ring alive.

Tyrone cocked his head, leering. "If you think you can dodge this—forget it!" He clicked his tongue. "Do you know what happens if they see that you don't give it all you have? They'll give you away as a . . . well, how do they call it? A *toy*, I think. Well, that's the word the Player uses. You know him? The man with the scars on his face? He calls the shots here." He stepped closer, lowering his voice. "Ever heard of humans being sold for money? Welcome. You've entered the world of crooks who'd sell their mother for a decent buck."

Thomas retreated to the rear of the cell. He wished for Tyrone to leave him alone, but the Turner offspring continued blathering about the fights, the tormented men, and how bloody they looked when they were taken out of the ring to be replaced with new fighters for the entertainment of the rich company bosses, who could afford to spend thousands of dollars for their pleasure. Obviously, Tyrone enjoyed being a part of the illegal game, of having contributed a fighter for the masses. The plan was as simple as it was cruel.

"This wasn't your idea," Thomas said. "It was Jebediah's."

"How — ?" Tyrone pressed his lips tight, growling. "Okay, but how did you know?"

"You're too stupid to find your ass in the dark. How would you come up with a plan and the means to conduct it? It's a pity Jeb's not here to see me, isn't it?"

Tyrone pressed his face against the bars. Spittle flew with his words. "I'm here to see you, asshole! I'm here to laugh when you hit the floor face first! I'm here to watch your bones being broken!" He banged the bars. "And I will get my cousin free, one way or another!"

With two steps, Thomas was at the bars and smashed his fist through the gap, hitting Tyrone's face with enough force that the gangster retreated with a bloody nose.

"He'll rot in prison!" Thomas yelled. "We all testified to what we watched. And I bet the evidence will link him to the murder of Milton Roker. Am I right? *Am I right?*"

"No! You miserable fucker! *I did this!* I guided his hand when he was too squeamish to push deeper. And you damn well know it!" Tyrone held his bleeding nose, and his voice cracked more the louder he spoke. "I'm the one who's got the guts to do this! Jeb was way too soft for this kind of job. I took care of Snakey and called Michael to take him away. That was *my* decision. Jeb was gone, tangoing with the toilet."

Thomas leaned against the sidewall and let out a big breath. He felt helpless and isolated. Tyrone's confession was worthless until taken to a judge, and there was a snowball's chance in hell the criminal would ever see a cell from the inside unless Thomas could break down the door, grab Tyrone, and drag him back to Washington after killing all the guards on the compound. The image was tempting.

Fighting despair, Thomas laughed.

Tyrone looked as if he'd crack the bars to get in. "What's so fucking funny? You'll fight and you'll die!"

"Unless I can convince a rich guy to bail me out and take me home."

Tyrone's face fell. His lips parted, and his look told Thomas that he hadn't considered that solution. Tyrone spat. "You'll *die*, asshole! You will die, and my laughing face will be the last you see!"

The open-plan office was always filled with low murmuring of agents on duty, either in conversation or on the phone. When the background noise rose to a distinct chatter, Nicolas lifted his head to search for the reason. His eyes widened upon seeing Lesley strut along the main aisle, straight in his direction.

Compared to her usual outfit, Lesley Gilbert had chosen conservative apparel consisting of high heels and a tight black dress that featured a low décolleté. Her red lipstick and black-framed eyes spoke of her intention to stand out. Her long hair was styled into an elegant bun with two locks dangling at her cheeks, which danced with every step she made. Whenever she gave her languishing look to someone, the agents appeared to hold their collective breaths.

"Holy moly," Jason whispered. His eyes and mouth were wide open. Like the other men in the room, he couldn't take his eyes off her.

Nicolas stood to greet her. "Hello, Miss Gilbert, what brings you here on this sunny day?"

Lesley dropped her woolen coat across the table, barely missing a coffee cup. Her voice and look were serious. "I need to talk with you. Right now. No excuses." She pulled herself a chair out and sat down. Her gaze said he'd better follow her order or her anger would hit him harder than a whip.

Nicolas decided to withstand the urge to do her bidding. "May I introduce my partner to you, Jason Beckham?"

Jason hurried to reach out for a handshake. "Pleased to meet you."

Lesley ignored him, and when Jason didn't waver, her gaze hit him cold as ice. "Get lost."

"Excuse me?"

Nicolas needed a second to find his voice. "Lesley, please, this is my place, not yours. What's so important?" He looked up to find most of his fellow agents standing in their booths to get a glimpse at the visitor. "Come on, I'll take you to the cafeteria. We can't talk here." He pulled her up from the chair.

"It's important. Don't try to shoo me out." Lesley broke the grip. "And don't ever touch me again."

"All right. Let's go." Nicolas took the shortcut to the stairs and chose a table at the far end of the cafeteria. When Lesley sat down, he asked, "Can I offer you something? Coffee? Tea?"

"I'm here to ask you for a favor. Sit and listen."

Nicolas sat down on the other side of the table and smoothed his tie. He felt an itching along his arms and back and his pulse quickened. "What's the problem?"

Lesley put her hands on the table. Her nails were a deep red, matching the lipstick. She looked him deep in the eyes and lowered her voice. "Nick, you've got to do something for me."

"Let's see if I can help."

"My friend told me that two of her most frequent customers haven't shown for three weeks, another one for four days." She lifted a hand to stop him from answering. "Yes, I know. The police say they probably left the city, changed jobs, didn't want to come to the dungeon anymore. She's heard it all. But the last one I mentioned owns a classic 1967 Ford Mustang and guess what—it's still at the parking lot behind the dungeon."

Nicolas frowned. "The police didn't consider this odd? Are they investigating?"

Lesley rolled her eyes. "Not according to my friend's statement on the phone. The officers didn't take her seriously. You know our business doesn't have the best reputation. Many people need it, but no one wants to know about it. We're working in a gray area." She waved her finger *no*. "But that's not the point. I want you to investigate these cases of missing people—of *kidnapped* people. I'm convinced they didn't leave the city but were forced, one way or another."

"It's not my division, Les. Honestly, your friend cannot prove what happened. They could be in town, they could've moved, or maybe the one with the Mustang fell sick and couldn't claim his car."

Lesley's eyes narrowed as she pressed her lips together. "You don't want to help me? Is that it? You've got the entire FBI behind you, and yet you sit here and tell me you can't do a fucking thing?"

Nicolas lifted a hand to stop her tirade. "First, this can't be an FBI case unless the kidnapping is proven in any way. Even if the men were kidnapped, it's not *my* case. I work violent crime—serial killers, bank robberies, and other cases with a high potential for violence. The FBI has another division for kidnapping cases."

She made an impatient gesture. "Then talk with them. I don't care, as long as someone investigates."

"Are there any connections between the men? Job? Private life? Hobbies—aside from visiting the dungeon?"

"Well, for one, the dungeon visits are a connection. And they look alike." She made a face and gestured with her hands. "Not in the sense of brothers or other relatives. But Ursa told me they are young, tall, muscled — men who draw attention wherever they go. As far as she knows, they're single and don't have much besides their visits at the dungeon."

"Is Ursa really her name?"

"No, probably not, but she likes the sound. Not to mention that Ursa was one of the enemies of Superman." Lesley's smile vanished as quickly as it appeared. "Does that help? Will you take the cases to your division?"

"The police —"

Lesley hit the table with her palm. Her brown eyes held the fierceness of a mistress, and Nicolas didn't doubt she would act out if he found no way to stop her. "Are you deaf? The police have already reached their verdict. They won't do anything unless we find proof that these men didn't just vanish. How many cases do you need to call it a *serial kidnapping*?"

"I was going to say that I'll ask the police for the files. After that, I'll talk with my colleagues and see whether there have been other cases of presumed kidnapping, okay? I won't promise anything. Your friend should keep her eyes open in case one of the men shows up. I don't want to make a big deal out of this and learn that it was all a misunderstanding. Do you understand that?"

Lesley's frown reappeared. "We know our customers. In cases like these, we know the men better than they know themselves. For them, coming to the dungeon is an addiction. They come back like a drug addict returns to his dealer. They wouldn't stay away without a word."

Nicolas put his elbows on the table and met Lesley's gaze. It was on odd situation. Even though she wasn't his mistress, she had participated in several love nights he had spent with Jacklyn. She knew of his own addiction and how his relationship with Jacklyn had evolved over the years. Her expression made his skin crawl, but he got a grip and remained professional. "I need the contact to Ursa."

Lesley pushed a calling card across the table.

"Okay. I need all details you have about the men."

"Ursa will tell you what she knows. I told her that you understand the business much better than others." Once more, Lesley's smile was short-lived. "She'll treat you like an insider."

"Fine. I want you to reach out to other dungeon owners." Nicolas resisted her influence with all he had. "Ask around. If there's a pattern, there's a chance to catch the criminals before they select other victims." He let out his breath. "I won't promise anything. Really, Lesley," he said when she stood. "DC has a high turnover—people move here for a job and leave if their expectations fail. Unless there are tangible hints at a kidnapping, the FBI division won't take over the investigation."

"It's better than nothing." Lesley put a hand on Nicolas's shoulder, and her smile was warm and grateful. "I'm counting on you."

Nicolas watched her leave and wasn't surprised that in her wake, two men dropped their coffee cups and another one cursed as he sprayed ketchup on his shirt.

"Listen, Agent Lawry, I know you've got better things to do than answering my questions, but—" Nicolas hesitated. On the way to the FBI division dealing with kidnapping cases, his request had appeared sound. Right now, he feared he'd embarrass himself in front of the stunning blonde agent with the large blue eyes.

She looked at him expectantly.

Though he wasn't hesitating because of her breathtaking appearance, her smile indicated that she knew how her looks affected people. She wore little make-up and small golden earrings, matching her elegant suit and white blouse. "A friend of mine is worried because three young men vanished from a dungeon in DC within three weeks."

"Go on."

"The men were of similar height and build, young, agile, single. I wondered whether there are similar cases you're already dealing with."

Agent Lawry nodded and turned to a large-scale map of the city. "Where exactly?"

Nicolas gave her the address, and she used pins to mark the spot.

"Hmm, three more." She turned to him and gestured toward a pile of files on the left side of her desk. "Eleven cases within six months, and that's only the larger DC area. We're in constant exchange of information with the other field offices, but so far, the cases are concentrated on the east coast — DC, Boston, New York."

"Big cities with a high number of potential victims."

She sat down at her desk. "That's right. Give me the details."

Nicolas handed her the files he had received from a grumpy police detective. "I haven't had time to talk to the dungeon owner, Ursa."

Agent Lawry nodded as if this interrogation could wait and quickly checked the contents of the file.

Nicolas looked at the pins on the map. "The other men were of the same age and physique?"

"Yes." Agent Lawry nodded while she copied the data into her computer file. She was the fastest typist Nicolas had ever seen. "We'll check their apartments, cars, workplaces." She looked up. "The victims are male, young, in good shape, and they either visited sex shops or other erotic places, including dungeons." She pointed toward a whiteboard with pictures of the victims. "So far, we know the men were alone at the time they disappeared, and that they have no relatives or good friends in town. The missing person reports came in from neighbors or employers, but by that time, the victims might've been gone for three or four days. We're way behind the kidnappers."

"What do you know?"

A small frown line appeared on her forehead. She stood to pin the pictures of the latest victims on the board. "It's a definite pattern. The men are alone on their way to their cars or to their apartments. No one misses them instantly. The kidnapping must be done professionally, because four of the men have training in martial arts and would know to defend themselves against a gang of robbers." She pushed up her sleeves. "We assume it's a group of four to six armed men with experience. Probably the men had no time and no chance to defend themselves but were taken away quickly. I assume they use drugs to make their victims comply without much resistance."

Nicolas thought of Thomas's kidnappers but held back this information. "Who kidnaps young men? For what reason?"

Agent Lawry's brows twitched. "I could list a lot of statistics, but let me tell you this—every year, more than fifty-seven thousand people vanish in the US—kidnapped or lured away. They end up in prostitution, forced labor, or as organ donors."

Nicolas shuddered involuntarily.

"That's right. The highest percentage of those crimes is connected with forced prostitution, but if you think prostitution is limited to female victims, you're wrong. Statistics say that half of the victims are men, but that's not proven, since many men don't come forward even if they escape their captors. The same goes for victims of forced labor. While the women are forced to clean houses or sew pretty clothes in sweatshops, the men are misused in agriculture or the packing industry. If you want another statistic, take this — reputable agencies estimate up to forty million men, women, and children are enslaved and trafficked around the world *today*. Slavery isn't a story of the past. It's an enormous business with increasing profits."

She cleared her throat. "Since the enactment of the Trafficking Victims Protection Act in October 2000, the US government and executive agencies have undertaken massive efforts to fight those crimes. TVPA strengthens domestic criminal laws against human trafficking and forced labor, but it's only an effective instrument if enforced." She cast him an apologetic glance. "I could go on like this, but it doesn't change the situation. Fact is, we're dealing with a highly organized criminal organization that's operating across state borders with sufficient connections to other gangs — the mob or similar — and enough men bearing arms to withstand prosecution or start a war."

"That doesn't sound like a crime that can be solved in a few days." Nicolas stared at the board with the photographs. "If you showed me these pictures without the background, I'd say they either sent their pictures to appear on a model magazine cover or to prepare for a tournament. Do you think they were lured by quick money for fights?"

Agent Lawry checked the information she had about all the victims, then nodded. "Three of them are in serious trouble and have little or no money. The others have jobs and pay their debts." She lifted her gaze. "Three cases could fit this theory. Judging by the looks of it, a few of them might've accepted an invitation from a modeling agency and were lured with money and fame. As for the others — we don't know enough about them to judge their characters."

"What does the profiler say?"

Agent Lawry rolled her eyes. Her tone indicated she wasn't

satisfied with the profiler's report. "A group of professionals takes the men to a hidden location. They vanish and don't re-appear, not even their bodies—assuming any of them were killed. We don't know that. The profiler says this pattern rules out a serial killer, because such criminals work alone, and they tend to show their bodies to the public. He assumes there is an organization behind the crime, whether it be for forced labor, sex, or organ exploitation. That fits with age and gen-der. Whereas I tend to assume they were kidnapped for pros-titution, because their looks are outstanding. No criminal would go to that trouble if he just needed a few farm work-ers." She called up the list of characteristics and let Nicolas have a look. "It's terrifying how many victims they've found so far."

"We've got a high-risk group, but can't warn them effec-tively, because where they go, they want to be alone."

"Excuse me?"

Nicolas rubbed his chin. "They were at places where they go alone. You don't want company when visiting a dungeon or an erotic theater. It would be awkward." When Lawry raised her eyebrows, Nicolas went on. "If I read it right, five of them were new to the city, others have lived here for a few months but are single and haven't connected to another group of people yet. You wrote under two photos they were *loners*. The kidnappers don't have to look far, but they do research, obviously. They're not randomly attacking a victim in the street."

"That's correct. Your report of three more victims indicates that they concentrate on men frequenting sex shops. We can't warn them and—to be honest with you—we can't supervise all the dungeons and shops of various kinds, not even in DC."

"But you could warn the businesses so that they increase their security staff."

"Oh, really?" She laughed. "The high-prize establishments

might do this, but the many small shops can't afford security measures. Most of them don't even have video surveillance."

"What's your countermeasure?"

"We did send out warnings to all shops and dungeons along the coast when the first victims were reported, but as long as we don't have tangible hints at the kidnappers, we have no choice but to look for clues within the victims' personal surroundings." She read his disappointment. "We can't issue a global warning to all men who look like this that they shouldn't walk alone. We'd either cause a panic or warn the kidnappers, and they'd do their business elsewhere."

"Back to the unknown location, Agent Lawry."

"Christina."

"Nicolas."

"I know."

Nicolas hid his confusion about her warm smile and looked back at the pictures. "You assume the men are being kept somewhere. Since they're growing in numbers, you can't hold them hostage in an apartment or a house in the suburbs. You need a large remote area with buildings where you can keep prisoners until they're taken elsewhere."

"Sold, for example. Or used for illegal fights, if I follow your idea."

"Right. What do you have about suitable estates, either along the east coast or farther to the west?"

"I learned that such organizations don't work within a hundred-mile radius. If they have a headquarters, it'll be far away from DC and New York so that victims and kidnappers can't be connected. You need a lot of acres, far away from towns where people would watch their doings." Christina smiled wryly. "Imagine the neighbors witnessing boxing matches in a garden. Or watching people taken away in handcuffs so that they can't cause trouble. Wouldn't make such a good impression, huh? So we're looking for a remote area outside of town where normal people don't go—an old estate, a large farm, an industrial complex that's been left to rot for years. Unfortunately, these types of accommodation are numerous, even if we rule out the ruins. Even with help from local authorities, we can't check them quickly. It'll take time, and there's a chance that if the kidnappers find out about our investigation, they'll either transport their victims elsewhere or kill them and vanish."

"Do you expect the kidnappers are bribing local police or politicians?"

"Yes. In most cases, the leader of such an organization is a respectable man, pays his taxes, and shows a reliable face to the public. He knows important persons of the county and bribes them or blackmails them, whatever works." Christina shook her head. Her blue eyes expressed deep sympathy. "I'd like to help you, Nicolas, but the way it looks, the only relief I can offer is that the three men will be considered victims of the same kidnapping ring. They're no longer neglected."

Nicolas hesitated, still looking at the pictures. "It might be farfetched, but a friend of mine was kidnapped five days ago. He doesn't fit the profile one hundred percent, but I'd like you to add him to the list, just to be sure he isn't omitted."

"Why?"

Nicolas shrugged. "Call it a hunch."

"I've seen the movie. You match Russell Crowe's voice quite well." She twitched her brows. "All right, give me the details and why he doesn't fit."

Nicolas recited all information he had on Thomas's kidnapping, including that he had been taken away by a trained group of six men.

Christina took down notes, then turned to him, frowning. "He's too old."

"And he's not a loner. I bet he never set foot in a sex shop, either." Nicolas's small smile died. "I know, but the other criteria match. That's why I want him on the list."

Christina bit her lower lip. "Excuse my doubts, but his kidnapping sounds as if it is the result of a more personal feud. Nevertheless, I'll treat him like one of the cases I'm already working on. I'm connected with the ATF anyway, and they'll have a special interest in finding him on the list."

"Really?"

Christina went on. "The FBI offices work with the ATF, the Department of Justice, and several victims' organizations that help people freed from their captors. Exploited people need help to take up their lives again. As stated, many of them don't have friends, a home, or relatives they can turn to. We have many cases in which the missing person's report is filed by the employer." She frowned with sympathy. "I can't believe how many people in this country live alone, really alone."

Nicolas cocked his head, smiling tentatively. "But you're here to help find them."

"Oh, yes, that would be a great leap in my career." She lowered her gaze for a moment and pushed a strand of hair behind her ear, then parted her lips as if to start a sentence, but reconsidered to finally say, "I volunteered for this division, and I hope we can help these men and find the mastermind." She put a hand on the pile of files. "It's hard to understand that there are criminals ruthless enough to exploit victims in any possible way without feeling remorse or anything at all. They're just interested in the money." She let out her breath. When she continued, her voice was businesslike. "Let's talk with the woman named Ursa and hope that she'll cooperate." Making a face, Christina took her handbag and her car keys. "I heard that those dungeon queens are a strange folk."

CHAPTER FIVE

Thomas loathed that he couldn't push Tyrone across the railing to kill him on the spot. First, a high metal fence behind it prevented anyone from falling to the bottom. Second, Thomas belonged to the group of men handcuffed and connected with chains to each other who were about to be taken to the fighting arena Miguel had spoken of. Tyrone, this time dressed in an expensive dark red leather jacket and tight-fitting black jeans, strolled along the row of fighters, rambling about the quality of the other trained boxers and how quickly Thomas would lie on the floor and bleed to death.

"You have no chance, none, *nada*." Tyrone pulled up his nose and stroked his brown, unkempt hair out of his face. "The one you'll fight—he's got hands as big as plates."

Thomas bit down hard because he couldn't reach Tyrone's throat and throttle him. The chains between the handcuffed men were way too short, and the guards didn't allow the men to dawdle. The procession went downstairs and into the waiting van.

"I'll wait in the first row!" Tyrone announced when the doors closed. "And I'll be dancing when you die."

It was quiet inside the van—no one looked forward to fighting the man sitting next to him, so they all refrained from idle chatter. Thomas hung his head. It galled him that Tyrone was so close and that he couldn't bring him to justice. During the past three days, he had been thinking about how Tyrone had escaped the combined forces of the ATF and FBI that day.

Though he hadn't seen any Mexican drug lord in Tyrone's wake, it was the most logical explanation that the Turner off-spring had connected with his former partners to form a new alliance. When the Mexicans expanded their business, Tyrone had offered himself as a willing helper. He was as sly as he was brutal — traits the drug lords understood and cherished. Thomas didn't doubt Tyrone's willingness to prove his value, even by killing enemies of the cartel.

His musing was interrupted when the van stopped. The doors opened, and the fighters were led out in single file, straight into a large cage where the handcuffs came off.

Thomas was overwhelmed by the sight of the large arena, big enough to host about two hundred people. The hall was designed like one of the old boxing arenas of the thirties, when it was a national sport. There were flags and pictures of legendary boxers on the walls. Large spotlights illuminated the boxing ring and the galleries.

The atmosphere was heated, the chatter loud enough to drown the background music. There were about a hundred people around, dressed in suits and ties. A minority had come in casual jeans and pullovers, but no matter their outfits, they looked like the local upper crust, and many men appeared to know each other. They were chatting, drinking champagne or beer, and when the fighters came into view, they whooped with joy. Further away from the brightly-lit ring, guards were on patrol — armed but discreet — and waiters delivered fresh drinks and appetizers. Inside the boxing ring, a referee checked the floor and tested the ropes, just like any referee would do prior to a regular match. If Thomas hadn't known better, all details indicated that the audience was waiting for a legal entertainment.

Though he had seen a lot, Thomas was disgusted by the enthusiastic crowd. He couldn't understand how people willingly engaged in a spectacle they knew was felonious. But was it? The scarred man could reassure the audience that all fighters had signed contracts and were treated fairly. None of the fighters in the cage was haggard or appeared close to collapsing. It was the bitter truth — if the boss wanted, this venture looked legitimate, maybe with a touch of ruthlessness, but never like the venture of a criminal mind.

Thomas recognized Tyrone standing close to the fence. With him were two Mexicans, dressed for an evening at an exclusive club, including expensive watches and gold-rimmed sunglasses. When Tyrone gestured in Thomas's direction, the men turned their heads and curled their lips into malevolent smiles.

Thomas wasn't surprised that the guard picked him first and ordered him to step out of the cage. He handed him a mouth guard and boxing bandages, and when Thomas had put them on, led him to the center.

"For the first time and on his first fight night, we welcome Thomas!" the referee announced via loudspeakers. "He's an experienced fighter with lots of prizes back home. He's trained in different techniques and shouldn't be underestimated!"

Thomas heard the cheering crowd from afar. He was close to retching. He wanted to shout at them that he had been forced into this fight and that the spectators were all bound to be punished by the law, but then he glimpsed a man whose face he had seen on TV. In all probability, there were also local politicians involved, and even the local sheriff might turn a blind eye. Thomas's stomach churned. He had mulled over his approach the entire day, and now that his opponent entered the ring, he knew he had no chance to dodge the fight and come to an agreement.

"And on the other side, there's Alonso! He's proven his value in numerous fights and turned out the winner every time! Welcome, Alonso! Remember, it's time to place your bets. As soon as the bell sounds, no bets will be accepted."

The Mexican had the physique of a professional wrestler with arms beefier than some women's thighs. Judging by the look in his eyes, he was determined to win this fight as well. He bared his teeth, lifted his arms to the crowd, and enjoyed the cheers.

Thomas rolled his head left and right, loosened his shoulders, and feverishly thought about a strategy that would keep Alonso from killing him with a single blow.

The Player was annoyed about leaving the arena the moment the first fight began, but the caller's identity forbade any delay. He left for the quiet corridor, shooed two guards out of his way and took the call. The Chinese businessman on the line spoke with a heavy accent, but most of his words were understandable.

"I call you on behalf of Mr. Cheng," the Chinese man said slowly, as if he were selecting the English words one by one. "He asks you whether he might make use of your service to acquire an object that is most important to him."

The Player understood that Mr. Cheng had—not for the first time—seen a man he wanted to possess. Mr. Cheng was a rich executive with a special taste, living in the US because the country allowed businesses like his to flourish. Since he had come to know the Player, he had acquired handsome men for entertainment. "I can assist in the acquisition, but I need to know who we're talking about and where my men can find him."

"The object is located in Washington, DC. Mr. Cheng is willing to pay double the price of the usual merchandise under the condition that the object is taken without damage."

The Player lifted his brows. The request was a surprise. Usually, the customers didn't mind a black eye or bruises that were caused by the kidnapping team. Overwhelming an object without any harm was an art. "If that's a condition, I will have to stock up my team. That'll take a few days."

"Mr. Cheng agrees with your timetable," the man said after a minute.

The Player listened to the details, and when he ended the call, he sent for Kevin to have the kidnapping planned. This would be an outstanding job for his most reliable man.

Mistress Ursa, owner of the dungeon *The Lady's Lair* and two exclusive erotic shops with theaters, wore a black patent leather suit with a high neck and a long zipper down to her crotch. She was in her mid-forties, had red hair that framed her face to the best advantage, and wore stylish makeup with false lashes and an artificial beauty mark. Nicolas bet that without the dominatrix attire, she could pass as a businesswoman. She had — for all that mattered — the right demeanor.

Ursa's gaze was as intense as a laser beam, and Nicolas felt undressed. When she scrutinized him the way only a dominant woman did, Nicolas realized that Lesley had told her more than that he was an *insider*. He doubted that it had been a wise idea to join Agent Lawry.

He cleared his throat and unfolded his badge. "This is Agent Lawry, and I'm Agent Hayes. We're here to ask you a few questions about the missing men you reported."

Ursa lifted her chin and checked Christina up and down. Her look was condescending. "I don't waste my time with people who don't believe my words. The police sergeant demonstrated that he wasn't the least interested in my observations. What about you, Agent Lawry? Are you willing to listen and credit my statement, or are you here to do a tedious job and leave as quickly as possible?"

Nicolas started to put her in her place, but Christina made

another step into the waiting room. Her voice was business-like.

"Miss Ursa, the FBI has fourteen cases of possible kidnappings so far, including the three men you reported missing. I'm far from considering my visit a tedious job. I want you to tell me every detail you know about your customers so that I can adjust the profile I have of the kidnappers." She pointed toward a group of chairs and a small table in the center. "Can we sit down?"

"We can." Ursa glanced at Nicolas. "What's your position in the investigation?"

"I'm here because Lesley Gilbert asked me to support the case. That's what I do."

"Very well." They sat down. Ursa handed Agent Lawry a tightly written sheet of paper. "That's what I know about them — or what I observed. As you can see, I took down their credit card numbers so that you can check whether they used their cards after they didn't show up at the dungeon at the appointed time."

Agent Lawry's surprise was genuine. "That's . . . much more than I thought you'd have."

"If you treat this professionally, so do I."

Agent Lawry nodded, smiling. "Did they tell you everything about their lives?"

Ursa simpered. Once more, her glance hit Nicolas with full force, sending shivers down his spine. "Believe me, child, the men don't talk that much."

Nicolas felt heat creep up his face. Agent Lawry turned her head, and her surprise rose a notch. "Is there something I should know?"

"No." He couldn't look at her.

Ursa leaned back and quashed a smile. "I wrote down my observations and what I remember about their daily lives. Men aren't chatterboxes, but they share what they can't keep to themselves — and that's more than bragging about their assets."

"Their assets?" Agent Lawry looked at Ursa for an explanation.

"Their genitals. Men usually stress what they have, may it be with tight pants or by putting their thumbs into the pockets as a clear sign to where women should look. Men still think they define themselves by the size of their penis. If nothing else, they brag about how many women they've laid."

"Good to know."

Nicolas wanted to leave the room when Christina looked at him with new interest.

Ursa twitched her brows. "Roman came to me because normal sex bored him, and he wanted to come to know something new. I introduced him to several techniques. When he was satisfied, he revealed that he didn't like to go out, had no friends, and had no one he could talk to about his experiences. He was searching for a girlfriend but didn't know how to make the first step." She shrugged, smiling. "I gave him advice, but as far as I know his efforts had not yet borne fruit." Once more, Ursa rested her gaze on Nicolas. "More than a few men prefer a tough hand. They want the woman to dominate them, but that's nothing they can mention on a first date."

Christina looked utterly confused. She took down notes, but she appeared to mull over Ursa's words. "You mean he knew he wanted . . . a tough hand, so he returned to you frequently while he looked for a girlfriend?"

"Yes. As long as he didn't find a woman who understood his needs, he came back." She lifted her index finger. "Before you claim that he might've moved on to such a girlfriend, let me tell you that this kind of addiction doesn't vanish within a day. He would've returned if he had been able, girlfriend or no girlfriend. I can assure you that Roman is a character who would've told me — no, he would've proudly reported that he'd found a woman for his needs."

Christina added the information to the notes Ursa had made about Roman. "And the other two men had the same addiction?"

"Their needs differed, but spoken generally, they came to me to submit their bodies and let go of their daily responsibilities."

"What do you mean?"

Ursa crossed her legs and inclined her head. Frowning, she asked, "Have you ever thought about giving up control? Completely?"

"No."

Agent Lawry's decisive rejection made Ursa smile. "Men in leading positions face the challenge that even in bed they have to take control — they are expected to dominate the act of lovemaking. Giving up control is a possibility to enjoy sex in a different and most fulfilling way. Add some pain to the session, and you have a unique experience."

Her description as well as her voice spoke to Nicolas in such a way that he had trouble maintaining a blank face. His body reacted to the images Ursa planted in his mind. His heartbeat sped up, and no matter how hard he tried, he couldn't subdue the feelings. If Jacklyn had been with him, he would've have asked her to join him in one of the theme rooms the dungeon provided.

"Once a man finds out that he can reach a climax without stress, his love life will improve, and his action in the bedroom will be better, even if his lover doesn't dominate him every time."

"You're saying that men are under stress in bed?"

Ursa looked her in the eyes. "Men are always competing, even if there's no competitor in the room. They want to impress their partner and don't want to hear that the former lover was better, bigger, or more experienced." Ursa's brows twitched. "If you want to kill the mood, you can tell your new partner that the old one had the most impressive penis you ever saw. After that statement, you can leave, take a shower, and dress again."

Christina replied tongue in cheek. "I'll remember that."

"Is there anything else you want to know, child? You look like you've got a thousand questions on your mind." She bent forward, and her voice sank to a confidential whisper. "I can make an appointment with you and show you what you don't want to talk about."

Christina stood, a forced smile on her lips. "Thank you for your time, Miss Ursa. If we have any more questions, we'll contact you."

"Anytime." Ursa unfolded her legs and stood with the grace of a leopard. "I'm sure you have a calling card for me."

Christina handed her one, still smiling. "Here you go. The office is manned day and night."

"Thank you, Mistress Ursa," Nicolas said as he turned to leave.

She held him back at the sleeve and waited until Christina had passed through the door. "Your mistress trained you well," she said quietly. "But I bet that I could teach you some new tricks. I've got a science fiction and fantasy room—blue lights and fancy cuffs included."

Nicolas's mouth was dry. Thinking of being tied up in a semi-dark room, aroused by the shackles as well as his mistress's hot words, he was getting hard. He hated that Ursa had succeeded in manipulating him. He straightened and kept his voice down to business. "Listen, Ursa, I'm here as an FBI agent. You said that we should treat this professionally. You expect me to do the same, right?"

Ursa jerked back as if slapped. She broke eye contact. "You're right. My apologies. If there's anything you need, feel free to contact me."

"Agent Lawry is in charge of the investigation. *She* will contact you."

Nicolas took a deep breath once he was back on the parking lot. He felt as if he'd just surfaced from a deep lake. It was a cool day, and yet his dress shirt was damp with sweat. Although Lesley had told him that Ursa would be in the know, he had underestimated his own reaction. He slipped into the passenger seat, covering his erection with his winter coat. Christina put the key in the ignition but stopped to look at him.

"What the hell was going on in there?"

Nicolas knew it was useless to play dumb. "She's a dominatrix, and in her eyes, I'm prey."

"Just because you're a man? Don't gimme that crap." She started the engine.

"It's not crap. She's playing her part. She can't switch to a normal behavior with a snap of her fingers."

"Defensive, huh? Do you know more than you're telling me?"

Nicolas met her gaze, disliking the agent's inquisitorial look. "You interrogated her, she answered your questions, and you have the facts about the three men. Whatever more do you want?"

Her trimmed eyebrows twitched as she pursed her lips. He knew she wanted to ask more questions but decided against it. Slowly, with much skill, she filtered the car into traffic.

Thomas knew that his only chance to leave the ring on his feet was to avoid being hit at all costs. Alonso had mighty paws, but his brain was small. He trusted in his hooks—powerful punches, which, if they hit correctly, immediately sent the opponent to kiss the floor. The trick was to evade long enough to confuse him and then—with more luck than skill—hit him on a soft spot.

The theory was sound, the practical application a challenge.

Thomas danced around his opponent, nimble, quick, with a smile on his face. He bounced backward when Alonso stepped forward and punched his sides whenever possible. The man's fat layer was thick enough to absorb the hardest impact. Alonso grunted but didn't sway. Thomas feared that his tactics weren't working When Alonso struck out for another blow, Thomas kicked him in the genitals and blocked the man's right arm with his left. The impact was strong enough that his arm hurt as if it was broken, but that was nothing compared to Alonso's agony. The giant howled in pain and went down on his knees, holding his crotch.

Thomas stepped back, but when the referee didn't send him to his corner, he finished his enemy with a kick to his face. Alonso slumped to the floor and didn't move. Blood gushed from his nose and stained the canvas.

The audience stared in stunned silence. Thomas feared he had made a wrong move, done something that would take him straight to the killing zone, but then the crowd cheered, loud and enthusiastic. The referee took Thomas's right arm and raised it.

"Winner of the first fight tonight—Thomas! Congratulations!"

Thomas's left arm was throbbing with pain. He couldn't lift it anymore. While the cheers lasted, he was sent out of the ring. A guard took the mouth guard and the bandages. Another one shouted at him to hurry back into the cage. A man in white clothes with a large bag came running. He looked after Thomas's injured arm while the referee announced the second pairing. Thomas turned around to watch Alonso being dragged out of the ring. He hadn't regained consciousness yet.

Exhaling with relief, Thomas slumped on a bench. The doctor examined his left arm, stated it wasn't broken and declared he couldn't fight a second time that night because of a severe contusion. He applied salve and bandaged the forearm professionally, then left to report the result to a man standing next to the boxing ring. A brief conversation followed, and the guard in charge took down notes on a board.

Thomas leaned against the fence behind him. While the bell sounded for the second fight, he made eye contact with Tyrone. The young man's face was contorted, and he looked as if he would burst out of his skin, unable to keep the overbearing fury inside. Thomas lifted his middle finger in Tyrone's direction. It was a childish and idiotic gesture, but enough to make Tyrone explode like fireworks. He tried to push through the crowd, but one of the Mexicans held him back, angry as well as embarrassed. A heated discussion with much gesturing ensued.

Thomas imagined Tyrone was demanding his enemy's death on the spot, with any weapon handy. From Thomas's position, it was comical to watch the young flunky fight the stronger man's arms. The second man in charge slapped Tyrone's face to stop his babbling. When even that measure didn't help, he dragged him toward the exit.

Thomas greeted Tyrone with a mock salute. His arm hurt like hell, and he wasn't closer to an escape plan than he'd been hours ago, but at that moment, he was content.

Christina stopped the car two blocks away from the FBI headquarters and turned to Nicolas. "I want to apologize. You're right. I have no right to ask you questions. I got what I wanted, in fact I got more than I expected, because Ursa acted like a concerned citizen and not like a queen. Well, after the first two sentences."

"I'm glad she could help with your investigation." Nicolas pointed with his chin toward the street. "Is there a reason why we're stopping?"

"Yes, I wanted to apologize and invite you for a beer."

"Apology accepted." He smiled and shrugged his shoulders briefly.

"But you don't want a beer." Nodding, Christina pursed her lips. When Nicolas didn't say another word, she drove the car away from the curb again. "Does your lovely lady wait for you at home?"

"She does."

He could tell by Christina's quiet sigh, accompanied by a longing gaze, that she had expected to spend the evening with him.

She nodded toward the windshield. "Is it okay for you if I ask you to accompany me to another interrogation, especially when it comes to the owners of dungeons?"

"I'll accompany you, if you want me to, provided I have the time and no case of my own to take care of."

Christina huffed and tapped the steering wheel. "An agreement with a condition." She steered the car into a parking space in the garage and pulled out the key. "You said you know Lesley Gilbert." She looked him straight in the eyes. "She owns a dungeon in town. I've seen the advertising. You're friends with her?"

Nicolas opened the seat belt. "I know her."

They got out of the car. "Well enough that she tells you about the kidnappings and expects help from you?"

"Obviously." He closed the door. "What's your point?"

Christina made a dismissive gesture. "Just curiosity. I was wondering how a man like you gets to know a dungeon queen."

Nicolas jingled the keys for his car. "A good night to you, Christina." He walked away.

Chapter Six

While driving through thick traffic toward Lesley's dungeon, Nicolas calmed down. Christina would spend the evening alone, and he couldn't help but wonder why she'd been miffed about him declining the invitation. Did the attractive agent expect a man to comply, no matter his status in life? As far as he remembered, she had seen him with Jacklyn at the last Christmas party. He was astonished at Christina's behavior and was still mulling over women and their cryptic ways when he entered the lobby of the *Cave of Love*.

At this hour, the lobby was filled with men of all ages and backgrounds. He saw a fat businessman wearing a tuxedo and bow tie, a couple of young dudes in fancy clothes too restless to wait and pacing the room, and a Chinese man with thick glasses who held an attaché case on his lap and looked as if he'd break into a run any moment. His gaze was fixed on the counter as if he expected to be called to a doctor's appointment. To Nicolas's surprise, a group of three young Japanese women huddled around a table, giggling like teenagers and showing each other pictures on their smartphones. The men cast them irritated glances. In the far corner of the room stood a security guard, giving the impression of a no-nonsense person with the right to throw out misbehaving guests.

Nicolas walked straight toward the counter and was greeted with a hearty slap on his shoulder. He jerked and turned around.

"Hey, Nick!" Raiden grinned broadly. "Long time no see! Waiting for your girl?"

"Hello, Raiden." Nicolas needed a moment to collect his wits. "You're here to see your lady?"

"Yup. And you?"

"Jacklyn's at home. I need to talk with Lesley before you two get started."

"That doesn't sound as if you'd want to join us."

"Definitely not." He asked the receptionist for Miss Gilbert's whereabouts, and the young woman hesitated with her answer. Nicolas opened his badge briefly and in a way that no one else noticed. "Now, please."

The receptionist was clever. Her smile didn't waver. She pretended to check Miss Gilbert's current location and told Nicolas to walk straight toward the end of the corridor. "There's a dressing room to your left. She'll be there."

"Thank you." Nicolas turned to Raiden. "It won't take long."

"All right, I'm in no hurry."

Nicolas swiveled around when a glass tumbled across one of the small tables. The Japanese girls giggled louder, while the man with the attaché case was leaving with hasty steps. The security guard spoke into his headset, probably calling someone to clean up the mess.

Beyond the lobby, the light was dim, the conversations muted. It appeared that all rooms had soundproof walls and doors, so that Nicolas felt as if he was walking under water. At the end of the corridor, the conversations got louder, and he found the door to the dressing room halfway open.

He stopped in front of it. "Lesley?"

Inside, the laughter died away. "Yes?"

"Would you please, step out for a moment?"

"You must wait. I'm not decent. But you can come in, if you want to."

"I'll wait." Nicolas clasped his hands in front of his body and stepped aside when two mistresses in the tightest dresses that allowed them to breathe walked by, checking him up and down and making purring sounds. He was angry that they considered him a customer, even though they didn't know the reason why he'd visited the dungeon.

Lesley appeared five minutes later, wearing a black lace bra and long leather pants. The studded leather collar went well with her silvery hair decoration and the black belt. She checked the clock on the wall.

"I don't have much time. What do you want?"

"Raiden knows I'm here."

"Raiden's not the next one in line. He's always early and then keeps my receptionist from working." She smacked the crop in her palm.

"Okay. Agent Lawry and I spoke with Mistress Ursa today."

"Fine. I hope she could help you."

"What did you tell her? Did you tell her to try and seduce me? Or to embarrass me in front of a fellow agent?"

Lesley was quick with the crop, but he blocked her slap to his face.

"Not here, Les, and not now." He wrested the crop from her hand. "Answer my question."

"I told her you're a sub." She crossed her arms beneath her bosom and looked at him arrogantly. "Do you think she would've agreed to meet with you otherwise? The police already disappointed her. She wanted to make sure that *you* would listen to her." She reached for the crop, but Nicolas held it out of reach. "Yes, I might've told her that you're a trainee and that you have to learn a few tricks."

He made a step in her direction and hissed, "She offered me an hour in her fantasy room!"

"Wow, that's a unique invitation. Ursa's picky when it comes to clients."

"I don't consider this a compliment. Les, you asked me for

help because I'm an FBI agent, not because I'm Jacky's sub. So this was a professional appointment, not for fun. It was embarrassing, to say the least."

Lesley made a contented sound in her throat. Though she tried not to, she smiled. "So, she had you aroused by her speech. Not bad."

"It was bad enough, because the investigation is led by Agent Christina Lawry. She had some questions for me afterward that I really didn't want to answer."

Lesley cocked her right eyebrow and said with mock sympathy, "Really, Nick, are you still trying to hide what you love? Don't be one of those boring people who claim that sexuality is restricted to bedrooms and must take place behind closed doors and in the darkness. You're a young man in your prime. Of course you like sex. And when a woman like Ursa fires your imagination, you react. That's natural and nothing to be ashamed of. Tell me, did Christina try to get close to you after your visit to Ursa's place?"

Nicolas was confused. He hadn't linked Christina's reaction to their visit to the dungeon.

Lesley laughed. "And here you go, my wonderful agent. Your reaction sent her hormones flying through the roof. She couldn't help herself. So, please, don't blame her for what she did. She was horny, and you could've laid her in no time."

Nicolas's anger mellowed. He was still angry that Lesley had given away intimate information, but no longer grumpy that Ursa had tried to play a game with him.

Lesley claimed her crop. "All right-y, Nick the Beast, next time I'll prepare you better. Not to keep little Nick from pushing through the fabric, but to keep you from being embarrassed by nature's most wonderful reaction." She stood on tiptoe to kiss his cheek and strutted toward a room down the corridor. "See ya!"

Nicolas hung his head as he put his hands on his hips.

When he looked up again, another of Lesley's employees looked at him with wide eyes and a gamy grin. He shook his head, turned on his heels, and left the dungeon.

Thomas lay down on the cot, pulled the cover over his body, and closed his eyes. The cell door was locked. He didn't understand the guard's comment. It didn't concern him. He had survived the first fight with precisely the injury that would hamper him sufficiently to avoid another one. Given the fear he suffered, he had made the best out of a dreadful situation.

His left arm throbbed so much that he couldn't sleep immediately. Around him, other fighters were taken back to their cells. Doors were locked, muted conversations followed and became background noise to Thomas's attempt to sleep. He couldn't tell whether he'd ever been so worn out in his life. He remembered missions as a soldier, but they seemed far away and, in retrospect, less exhausting and less dangerous than his current situation. If he didn't watch out, the Player would force him to fight again and again until he found a master.

He found a position in which the pain in his arm was tolerable, and sleep was about to pull him under when a metal bar was hammered against the cell door.

Alarmed, Thomas sat up. "What the—"

"You're still fucking alive!" Tyrone shouted at the top of his voice. "You kicked that moron's ass, and *you, bastard, are still alive!*"

"His jewels, not his ass," Thomas said as he lay back and pulled the cover over his shoulders.

"You bested him, damn you!" Tyrone banged the door again.

Thomas bet the noise could be heard throughout the building. He closed his eyes, unwilling to argue with Tyrone, who was obviously drunk as a fiddle.

Once more, Tyrone vented his fury with the bar against the steel door. "Oh, now you're pretending to sleep? Shithead, don't you dare ignore me! Did you know? Jeb had decided to have you taken away by our Mexican friends after their next visit to collect the drugs they had stowed. You would've disappeared, and my dear grandpa would've heard a sad story about your decision to return to the big city from where you'd come." He laughed, loudly and hysterically. "My friends have been in the fight business for a long time. They always find men willing to step into the ring for a few bucks or some promises. The Player upped the game for them. Did you see all those people? They're *respectable* people. People who pretend to live a life by the rules of society. But here you see their true nature — they're all vultures, ready to rob the poor, ready to get horny watching the games. They call it entertainment, but that hides the fact that they know about the crime. And I tell you what — they don't fucking care!"

Tyrone shouted even louder. "No one in there is interested in the law or if mutual combat is allowed or not. They're getting off watching you and your opponent smash each other's faces. Then they place another bet and have a heart attack once their boxer wins." He scoffed. "Ah, the moment of victory. That's why they cheered you. No one had you on the list of winners. No one placed a bet on you." He clanked the bar against the door rhythmically. "But your luck won't hold. Next time . . ." He stopped. "Ah, the vigil's on its way." Thomas heard him step back from the door. "Am I interrupting your peaceful night? So sorry."

"Leave the wing now!" the first guard yelled at him. "If we see you here again, we have orders to throw you off the premises."

"Throw me off?" Tyrone laughed out loud. "I'm here with Juan and Arturo, the Player's best business partners. We're buddies, so to speak. So leave me alone, or you'll be the one kicked out. Okay?"

"They know you're here. That's why we were sent. Leave, or we'll use force."

Thomas lifted his head to see how Tyrone's arrogance faltered as he tried to save face. Nonchalantly, he threw the bar toward one of the guards before he turned and walked away with swinging steps. "See ya!"

Relieved, Thomas sighed and turned to sleep.

On the way home, Nicolas talked with Vernon on the phone to bring him up to speed concerning his joint venture with Agent Lawry and their visit to Mistress Ursa.

"Do you really think Tom was kidnapped for fights or being sold?" Vernon sounded incredulous. "I mean we suspected Tyrone and his flunkies, right? But kidnapped by a criminal organization—that sounds odd to me."

"The method is the same, and it's fair to assume that the Mexicans who dealt with the Turners are dealing with other gangsters on US soil. We don't know how many different ventures they maintain. If Tyrone made contact with them, he might've used his influence—"

"According to what Tom said, Tyrone alone is completely incompetent. He claimed that this man wouldn't find his ass in the dark. His words, not mine."

"Still, Tyrone escaped the police. He wasn't seen after the break-in at your home, which tells me he's able to stay off the radar."

Vernon needed a moment to digest the news. "All right, if he's with them, what's going to happen?"

"That depends on what the gang will do with him."

"Then find their hideout. Charlene's totally on edge. You can't imagine how she feels. She asks me every day whether there are any leads, and I have to tell her that the FBI is still looking for him." He sighed. "Bring him back, Nick."

"It's not my case, but the agent in charge has a very qualified team."

"But you said she's working on a case of serial kidnappings. What if Tom doesn't belong to them?"

"He will be found," Nicolas said, hoping he sounded convincing. "I'll keep you informed."

"Thank you."

With a heavy heart, Nicolas ended the call and drove home through the night.

Chapter Seven

As it was his habit, Raiden left the dungeon through the back door toward the parking lot where his *Chrysler* SUV waited. His plea that Lesley should take him home had fallen on deaf ears again. Without blinking, she had let him know that he was nothing more than a paying customer, restricted to pain and shackles in the dungeon. Not even his offer that he would stay as a pet at her home had changed her mind. Frustrated by her rejection and remembering what Nicolas had at home — it was heaven on earth — he pressed the key button that opened the car. He thought about stopping at a bar to drown his misery but decided against getting drunk. He had to work the next day and didn't want to anger Paul, who had swooned over a new and wealthy customer bringing a lot of money with him. Paul already had the dollar signs in his eyes, and Raiden was the last one to disappoint his partner. The prospect of yet another satisfied client driving off with a boat he designed lifted his mood.

When he opened the driver's door, two men appeared out of the shadow behind his car. He glimpsed the muzzles of automatic weapons. He dropped the keys and made a step back, then lifted his hands. "Hey! Cool down!"

The man next to him pointed the weapon at his chest. "Stop! Keep your hands up and don't move!"

Two more men came into view, similarly dressed in black combat gear with black hoods and thus unrecognizable by cameras. Their quiet and threatening moves seemed to be rehearsed, and he had no doubt about their intentions.

"What do you want?" Raiden shouted, loudly enough to be heard throughout the parking lot. "What's this about?"

"Shut up!"

He was pressed against the side of his car, handcuffed behind his back, and gagged so quickly he had no time to think further than his primal fear of being abducted for unknown reasons to an unknown location. His body rebelled and his adrenalin shot up, but his mind knew better. He wouldn't win a fight, and he didn't want to risk being shot if he had a chance to stay alive by cooperating.

A dark gray van backed up to where he stood. The rear doors opened, and Raiden was pushed inside. He had to sit on a bench, and one of the men locked a collar around his neck that was fastened at the wall. Raiden tore at the shackles, nearly throttling himself in the effort. The van left the parking lot while one of the men extracted a small syringe from his belt pocket. He changed sides and uncapped the needle.

Raiden retreated with wide eyes and tried to scream in spite of the gag.

"This will help you relax."

The needle sank into Raiden's neck. Contrary to what he expected, he didn't fall asleep. He noticed that his heart was beating more slowly and that he was calming against his will. His vision turned fuzzy around the edges, and a sudden urge to laugh surfaced. He bit the gag, trying to remain focused. He hoped Lesley would leave her club soon and call the police once she saw his car parked at the same spot. Raiden was optimistic about his mistress. She knew Nicolas Hayes. If one man could make a difference, it was the FBI agent.

The man with the syringe emptied Raiden's jacket and pants pockets and also took away his watch. Next came his shoes and socks. Even if he wanted to, Raiden couldn't find excitement in the man's eyes and realized his captors were doing this to control him and not to enrich themselves. These men were trained assassins, well paid and disciplined. Raiden wondered how he had become a target of such a professional group and for what reason.

Someone rapped on the door, loud and insistent. Nicolas opened his eyes. His alarm clock told him it was four o'clock in the morning. The rapping continued, so loud that Jacklyn, who had the healthy sleep of a bear in hibernation, turned, groaned, and mumbled about kids playing pranks.

"I don't think so." Nicolas wiped his eyes and tiptoed downstairs, convinced that Jacklyn would be asleep two minutes later.

"Open up! Please!"

Nicolas recognized the voice, but the urgency was most unusual. He opened the door, and Lesley hurried inside, tears on her cheeks and her hairdo a mess. She wore her dungeon outfit but shoes without heels. She clenched her handbag with both hands.

"He's gone! They took him! Nick, you've got to find him!"

Nicolas closed the door, took her by the shoulders, and led her to the couch. He put her handbag on the table. "All right. Who was taken?"

"Raiden!"

Nicolas made her sit on the couch and fetched a glass of water. When she refused, he knelt in front of her and took her hands in his. "Tell me what happened."

Lesley breathed loudly. He saw her effort to calm down and form words. "I left only minutes after him—I didn't want to meet with him again after we had a fight. Now I wish I hadn't been so stubborn. I found his car open and the keys on the ground."

He kneaded her hands gently and felt her trembling. "Did you call the police?"

"I did, right away. When I urged them, they sent for the FBI, and some people came to secure evidence. That's why I'm here so late. I wasn't allowed to leave in case they had more questions." She rolled her eyes. "Of course, they didn't find a fucking clue."

"Do you have cameras on the parking lot?"

"No, I don't. I never considered it necessary. My customers prefer privacy. Now I wish—"

"The gangsters would probably have destroyed them beforehand. They know what they're doing." Nicolas sighed. "Unfortunately, there's a criminal syndicate interested in men of Raiden's age and looks."

"No one looks like Raiden."

"Point taken. But the kidnap victims are young, muscled, have stunning looks, and they are single. All men were captured in isolated areas. They were alone, so there are no witnesses. I assume he was the last one to leave?"

"Yes. He stayed until after the last client had left." Lesley lowered her head, sobbing quietly. "You know, it's my fault."

"Your fault?" Nick crouched deeper to look into her eyes. "How could his kidnapping be your fault?"

"If I'd left with him as he wanted, he wouldn't have been taken away." She broke eye contact. "We had a fight. Not for the first time and . . . they've been getting worse from day to day. It started right after I brought him here for breakfast." She huffed. "I hadn't thought he'd make so much out of it. He begged me to take him home with me, to try something new. He offered that he'd be my pet and that I could tie him for the night so that I'd feel safe. I told him that I'd never take home a client, and he wanted to know if he was just a client for me or . . ."

She took a shaky breath. "He wanted to know whether there were no feelings involved. I refused to admit that I felt more for him than for any other man in the dungeon." She bit her lips as more tears rolled down her powdered cheeks. "He looked stricken. When I didn't take it back, he turned and left." Lesley reached for a handkerchief to blow her nose. "Honestly, I don't like to be pressured. I hoped he'd wait until I came to the conclusion that taking him home would be fun and not a . . . threat."

Nicolas remembered his conversation with Raiden. He should've known that the young man would confront her. "He waited a long time for you to say that."

She lowered the handkerchief, incredulous. "What do you know about him and me?"

"I know that he loves you, Lesley. He'd do anything for you." Nicolas sat back on the floor, shaking his head. "I'll talk to Agent Lawry, ask if she put him on the list."

"You're saying that he waited for me . . . that he endured everything I did with him because he hoped . . ." She shook her head, trying to compose herself. "No. I would've noticed that. I'm good at reading people."

"He hoped that you would feel the same for him." Nicolas shrugged. "He was mistaken. Obviously."

"You're piling guilt on my shoulders. That's really mean."

"Maybe, yes. We'll do everything we can to bring him back alive." He looked for his phone. "But the rest is up to you."

Lesley, the fierce mistress and ruler of her fate, looked as if she had been struck by a bullwhip.

The ride was so long, Raiden dozed in between and woke up when the van stopped. The collar was unlocked, and in the morning sunlight, the men led him across a large yard toward a three-sided building that appeared to be a former factory remodeled for a different purpose. Disregarding Raiden's weakness, they pushed him through a metal door and into a long corridor. In the center of a large area was a fenced boxing ring. Two stories up, rows with black metal doors as well as barred doors could be seen. Armed men patrolled the corridors, yelling at prisoners locked inside. Raiden saw several hands reaching out to the guards. He shuddered, thinking of being imprisoned for an uncounted time. He had never been to prison before. It was a nightmare come true.

He realized his kidnappers' viciousness when he was pushed into a small cell without a window.

"Kneel!"

Raiden was forced to the floor. Gag and handcuffs came off. One of the kidnappers locked the door from the outside before he could even ask a question. He was surrounded by darkness. Breathing raggedly, Raiden assessed the cell's contents and drank the water once he had carefully taken a sip. For half an hour, he sat on the floor, motionless, listening to the muted sounds outside.

The situation reminded him of a documentary about a prison in the Third World. He'd heard the reporter talk about poor conditions and that many prisoners died of malnourishment, injuries, and infections. It was said that prisoners were forgotten and died because the guards ran away. He didn't want to end his life as a casualty of someone's insane actions.

One more hour passed and nothing happened. Raiden had expected his captors to show up to beat him, interrogate him, even maltreat him in ways he didn't want to imagine. The negligence with which they had thrown him into misery and didn't pull him out again increased his hardship. He wished for something to happen, even if it was something bad. He was locked up—he tested the door twice—and couldn't see his surroundings. No matter his masochistic nature, this wasn't the pain he strove for. This was torture in the brutal sense of breaking a man's will to make him comply with the kidnappers' demands.

In the following uneventful hour, Raiden tried to pray,

something he hadn't done since his mother had taught him the Lord's Prayer. He prayed for patience, for a good outcome of the situation, and for help against his captors. The effects of the medication he had been given wore off. His anxiety grew into fear that made him tremble. When nothing happened and with the feeling that time was standing still, he hit the door, waited for the reverberations to cease, then hit it again until his strength reeled. He slipped down to the floor, devastated and filled with indelible panic that his captors would let him die of thirst and hunger.

His maltreated mind couldn't cope with a situation that had no safe word, no choice, no way to change the decision. Years ago, Raiden had been at a cruel master's mercy and suffered more than he should have at that time, but there had been a definite end both had agreed upon. In the end, he'd never set foot in that establishment again. He had never been locked up in a cage for more than an hour, and his mistress had been in sight all the time. It was a rule that a submissive was monitored during a session to help him or her in case sickness or injury occurred.

The safety instructions sounded like a joke.

Raiden was hungry. Before visiting the dungeon, he never ate much. Experience had taught him that a full stomach and a gag between his teeth didn't go together. Once and accidentally, a mistress had pushed him across a spanking bench so that he hit the rim with his stomach first. Raiden had tossed his cookies while the mistress stood in shocked silence.

Lesson learned.

Nicolas left Lesley in Jacklyn's caring hands, drove to the office, and requested a temporary transfer to the division dealing with the serial kidnappings. Senior Agent Sullivan lectured him about unwanted personal involvement and indicated that Nicolas wanted to be with Agent Lawry. In the next twenty minutes, he berated him about *acceptable behavior* and the unwritten rules at the office before he turned down the request but allowed him to join Agent Lawry should she request his presence. It was harder to explain the situation to Jason, who was angry, like a dog that had been denied his favorite treat. The only way to soothe his partner was to swear that he'd be there to help him choose his wardrobe for the wedding day. Though he wasn't confident that he could make it, Nicolas agreed to show up at the exclusive clothes shop at seven in the evening.

When he was back in his car, Christina called him. "Am I right in assuming you've been to Miss Gilbert's dungeon a few times before? If so, I'd like you to help me check the video surveillance of the lobby."

She must have seen him on the tapes. He didn't know whether he should try to explain or drop the subject. "I'll bring Lesley. She knows her customers best."

An hour later, Nicolas introduced Christina to a shaken Lesley Gilbert, who had reapplied her makeup but looked as if she was on the verge of tears.

Christina invited Lesley and Nicolas to sit down. "We checked the tapes for registered criminals. Facial recognition programs are good, but they can't replace the human eye." She pointed at the screen where men were sitting in the lobby. "I'm sure you can help us identify them, right?"

Lesley nodded. Her look was cautious. "You know, Agent Lawry, that my dungeon serves men and women of various backgrounds."

"If you indicate that there are politicians, police officers or even the DA among them, I can assure you I won't give any information to the press. What you tell me stays with me and my team. We aren't on a manhunt to compromise a politician's sexual preferences."

Lesley took a deep breath and pointed at the screen to identify the many men and a few women she knew were regular customers of her employees. Christina took down names and notes, lifting an eyebrow here and there when a famous name came up. Nicolas hadn't known, either, that Lesley Gilbert's venture had become so sought-after in such a short time.

"On the weekends, I've got a higher fluctuation and a few irregular clients who come while they are in town. Another small group here came and left without making an appointment. Obviously, they expected something else and decided against a visit." Lesley bit her lower lip. "I've got five ladies working for me. You can ask them whether they're able to put names to the remaining men I couldn't identify."

"Will do. Will they cooperate?"

"They will." Lesley's small smile bore sadness. "I don't know why you think people in the sex industry reject working with the police in general. We want to be taken seriously. You see that there's no doubt about Raiden's kidnapping. He wouldn't have left so suddenly to buy ice cream somewhere."

"I understand. And I don't doubt you," Christina said quietly.

"Wait a moment," Nicolas said, who had been staring at the screen the whole time. "This Chinese man close to the exit. Do you know him?"

"No." Lesley made a screen shot with her cell phone and sent it to her employees.

"He's been on three of the videos we watched so far." Nicolas pointed at him when Christina played back the video. "And there's Raiden. Different days, about the same time." He met Christina's gaze in a sudden revelation.

Christina nodded, smiling. "Let's check if he's on other videos where Raiden is, too."

"Raiden's a very regular customer," Lesley said. "He's in pretty much every video."

They spent half an hour skipping through the surveillance tapes and found four occasions in which Raiden and the Chinese man with the thick glasses appeared simultaneously.

Lesley asked Christina to stop the video they were watching. "Do you see? He's wiping his mouth. And he keeps his attaché case on his lap." She looked at Nicolas, then at Christina. "It's clear as day he's got a boner and he's hot for someone. If I have it right, there's Raiden standing and chatting with my receptionist. He always does that when he's early." She sighed. "I think the Chinese man was watching him. He's too agitated to be watching Cheryl. He can't see more than her head and shoulders."

Lesley's phone rang, and Cheryl reported that she had seen the man a few times prior to that day. He had made an appointment and cancelled it. The next time, he had claimed that he wanted to make an appointment for a friend, but he had cancelled that, too, a short time later.

Christina enlarged the image. "It's a start."

Lesley frowned. "What can you do with it? You said facial recognition doesn't work so well."

"He made a phone call, and because of the time stamp, we know when he made it. I'll contact the phone company and ask them for the phone records within the time frame." She shrugged. "It's no guarantee that we'll have a hit, but it's worth a try." She smiled encouragingly. "Whether you believe it or not, this is a tangible clue."

Lesley stared at the frozen picture. "Did he kidnap Raiden?"

"I doubt it." Christina used her hands to explain. "In a criminal organization like this, you have a group of men selecting the victims. They're on lookout, walking the streets, following the men around. We know that they do research, because they know their victims before they kidnap them. When the selection is made, they're looking for an opportunity. If they have that, the next step is to send the extraction team to overwhelm the victim and take him away quickly."

Lesley fought for composure, but her voice betrayed her. "You're saying he was overwhelmed within minutes?"

"That's right. Probably in less than a minute. According to Nicolas's statement about the kidnapping of Thomas Zutarski, the men are paramilitary experts, a team of six. They operate in perfect harmony so that the victim has no chance to defend himself."

"And he's not a fighter." Lesley's voice was small. "He's a swimmer, a navigator. He knows a lot about boats and design. He's a peaceful man." She took a deep breath. "Do you know of any reason why he was kidnapped?"

Christina gave Nicholas a worried glance.

"I assume that the victims are forced to fight," Nicolas said and took Lesley's hand. "That means he's alive and being kept somewhere. We'll work with the clues we have and tell you what we find."

When the door opened, Raiden was on the verge of crying. He had lost count of the time in the darkness. Squinting in the sudden brightness, he crawled out of the black hole, disorientated, bathed in sweat, and with his heart beating in his throat. Trembling badly, he wanted to beg his captors to never put him back in, but he couldn't make more than guttural sounds.

"Twelve hours, and he's a wreck," the guard beside him said, and kicked Raiden's side for good measure. "Get up, shithead!"

Raiden tried to find his feet, shading his eyes. He hurt all over his body, and the hunger came back with a vengeance. He lifted a hand in a weak attempt at gaining his captor's help. "I can't . . ."

"Get up, or I'll throw you back in!" the guard shouted in his ear. "Last chance!"

The threat fulfilled its purpose. Raiden put a hand against the wall and stood on wobbly legs, wheezing in misery. He lifted his gaze to find his captors staring down at him as if he were a beetle they would crush any second. One of them whirled a club in his hand.

"Please, I can't . . ."

"Go!" Another brutal push followed, and Raiden stumbled along the cells toward a tiled area with several showers. The installation looked newer than the rest of the building and quite clean. It was an oddity he noticed but didn't put into context. He wished he'd been someplace else the previous night. He wished he had a fighter's training and knew how to bash his enemies. He thought of Lesley and what she would do. And of Paul — that he would wait for him in vain.

"Out of the clothes!"

Raiden dropped his jacket and shirt. He wasn't squeamish when it came to displaying his body, but suddenly being nude equaled being vulnerable and helpless. He hesitated but took off pants and underwear when the guard made a threatening step in his direction. Raiden didn't know what their intentions were. Judging by their aggressive behavior, he expected the men to drop their pants and rape him one after the other. He was out of breath realizing he couldn't do anything to defend himself.

The second guard, a heavy man of about forty years with a thick black beard, pulled him toward one of the showers. "Stop." He used a collar that was chained to the wall to tether Raiden, then turned on the water. He gestured toward a bottle with shower gel. "Clean yourself up."

If it was possible under the circumstances, Raiden was grateful for small mercies when the guard stepped back and the tepid water ran over his body. When he turned, the first guard was filming him with his cell phone. Disgusted, Raiden faced the wall again, wondering about the reason and who would see the video. His initial fear that he was one step away from being abused came back forcefully.

"Turn around again. I need to see you from the front."

"What for?"

"Do you wanna go back in lockup?"

Raiden lowered his head, trembling again. No matter how much he hated it, he would comply, if only to avoid being thrown back into the black hole for hours. Slowly he turned around and rinsed his hair, aware of the collar that restricted his movement. Both guards were agitated. Raiden held his breath and watched them intently, ready to do whatever he could to avoid maltreatment. The one with the cell phone moved into the shower room to get a close-up.

"Get yourself hard."

"What? I can't." He pressed his back against the tiles and dropped his hands to the sides.

"You do what you're told, asshole."

Raiden closed his eyes for a moment, fearing the worst was yet to happen. "I can't because I'm wearing a restraint."

"Fuck this!" the second guard shouted and laughed out loud. "He's right!"

The first guard lowered the cell phone. "Damn it, Grotto, I hate this." He checked his watch, then shook his head, cursing viciously. "Go, get a key for this fucking lock. I'm on the clock." He put away the phone, plucked a pair of handcuffs from his belt, and turned off the water. "Hands behind your back. Don't make a move, or I promise I'll give you a thrashing you won't forget."

"Why are you doing this? Why are you making a video?" Raiden pulled up his nose. Now that the water was off, the stall was cool, and he shivered even more. "What do you want from me?"

"You're shaven, wearing a chastity device. What's your story?" The guard had small, dark brown eyes full of distrust and malevolence.

Raiden knew the type of guy — though of average height and build, his captor was strong and self-confident, especially with the club at his belt. He was a man who used his power to subdue others in any given situation. If Raiden was right, he had a taser gun in his holster. His breath smelled of mints when he pushed his chewing gum from one cheek to the other. "Come on, spill it."

Raiden tested the handcuffs. Though they were welcome on many occasions, he now felt cornered and miserable, on the verge of a panic attack. "I'm a submissive. My mistress wants me that way."

Narrowing his beady eyes, the guard made a disgusted sound in his throat. "You've got a woman dominating you . . . restraining you? You're a wimp?"

Raiden had heard that term before, but still the insult stung. "It's sex, but I can't explain it in a way you would understand, numbskull."

The blow into the pit of his stomach was the consequence, but didn't hurt any less.

"I'll teach you manners."

Raiden breathed against the pain. The collar around his neck kept him from doubling over. He would've throttled himself dropping to the floor. His voice was hoarse. "I bet you will."

Grotto returned with a small set of keys and opened the chastity device after a few minutes. The handcuffs came off again, and the first guard reached for his cell phone to switch on the camera again.

"All right, asshole, get a boner."

He twitched his brows with another evil grin.

Raiden understood that any resistance would lead him straight back to isolation and darkness.

Jacklyn hugged her girlfriend and led her into the living room. "I made tea for us."

"I'd prefer a shot of whiskey, if you don't mind. My hands are still trembling, and I can't think. That's no good."

"Shouldn't you stay sober in case the FBI needs your help?"

Lesley slumped on the couch and took off her shoes. "Are you getting mushy on me? I'll manage, okay?" She lifted a hand when Jacklyn hesitated. "I promise I won't empty the bottle. Get me a glass, please."

Jacklyn brought her a drink and put mugs and the teapot on the table.

"Thank you." Lesley drank and held the glass with both hands, staring at the table.

Jacklyn granted her time to think and busied herself in the kitchen. When she looked back, Lesley had refilled her glass and strolled through the living room.

"I don't have a picture of him. We don't take them in the dungeon for reasons." She looked up. "You have pictures all over the place. Of Nick and you. The last ones are from the housewarming party, right?"

"Yeah. My assistant took most of them. She's got the hang of photography. They're quite nice and catch the spirit of that day." She stood, remembering the day. "I'm glad we waited for the party until Nick was back. It would've been sad to celebrate without him."

"It's so strange. Raiden's been a customer for a year and —"

"Yes, a customer. Why should you have a picture of a *customer*?" she asked pointedly.

Lesley swiveled around. "What does that mean?"

Jacklyn wiped her hands on a towel, searching for words. "When you brought him here for breakfast—did you think of him as a customer, or more of a friend with extras?" When Lesley pressed her lips tightly together, Jacklyn nodded. "I assume you don't take other customers to see your friends, right?"

"Of course not. It was a unique opportunity. He loves being a pet, and I could take him with me without upsetting anyone. It sounded like fun." Lesley made a face. "I should've known that such fun's not welcome at your home."

Jacklyn ignored the accusation. "That's not the point. You call him a *customer* while you do things with him you don't do with others, even with some of your regulars you've known for years. Are you sure you don't have feelings for him?"

Lesley grimaced and turned away. "The scent of his aftershave was still in his car when I got there. I saw the keys and . . . His keys have that little pendant on them, a wooden wheel, the ones you have on ships."

Jacklyn crossed the room and hugged her friend from behind. "It's not your fault. Even if you had come out the door earlier, they would've taken him."

"It's coming back to me. The fight we had. The moment when he slammed the wall with his fist, grabbed his jacket, and stormed out. I thought he'd destroy the door. He was so angry." Lesley hung her head.

"He'd started coming to the dungeon more frequently, hadn't he?"

"Oh, yes. I thought—" Lesley made a helpless gesture. "It's irrelevant what I thought. I was so wrong. Fuck."

Gently, Jacklyn led her back to the couch, sat down beside her, and plucked the empty glass out of her hands. "This situation aside, what do you want from him? That he spend a lot of money?"

"You know better than that." Lesley took the teacup Jacklyn offered. "I told Nick that I was thinking about inviting him to my home, but . . . I wasn't ready yet. I didn't want him to push me. He's a nice guy, yes, but he's also someone who needs pain to be satisfied. In a way, he's quite a sicko."

Though she didn't want to, Jacklyn laughed.

"You're no friend today," Lesley scolded.

"Oh, yes, I am. I think I'm the only person allowed to contradict you. While you're saying he's a sicko, you want him to be *your* sicko. Don't deny it." Jacklyn waved a finger. "I know you too well. I also know you're picky when it comes to your place, your haven, your castle."

Lesley drank her tea and pursed her lips. "I shouldn't have told you so much about me."

Jacklyn nodded without agreeing. Though Lesley had never said it out loud, Jacklyn assumed her friend had suffered from domestic violence in her teenage years. While her mom had been a junkie with several equally addicted brutal lovers, Lesley had tried to stay out of trouble. Only when her mother left without a note had the Department of Children and Families tried to find her father. Though Mr. Gilbert had done whatever he could to give his daughter a home and education, he couldn't heal her psychological wounds. Lesley lived alone, pretended to have no desire for a lover, and avoided being with a man once he wasn't shackled. Occasionally, she acted as if the mere presence of one man made her uncomfortable.

"Your secrets are safe with me," Jacklyn whispered, putting an arm around Lesley's shoulders. "Will you be honest with me?"

Lesley lifted and dropped her shoulders with a heartfelt sigh. "Why not?"

"Do you want him to be with you for more than a session

at your dungeon?"

"That's an unfair question, considering that I don't know if he'll ever come back again."

"It's fair to come clean about your feelings, Les. It was obvious to me that Raiden wants you."

"He's too young. Look at the situation realistically. You're six years older than Nick, and you confessed that from time to time you have trouble because he doesn't understand you. You said that he appears to be a teenager while you're already an adult. What shall I say? Raiden's twenty-five, for god's sake. There are thirteen years between him and me. Right now, he finds me attractive, but in five years, he'll look at me and call me an *old lady*."

Jacklyn raised her brows, smiling, and patting her shoulder. "Yeah, right. That's a perfect reason not to start a relationship." She looked Lesley in the eyes. "What kind of tattoo does he have on his left arm?"

"It's a pattern made like a wristband. He had it done when he was sixteen."

"His parents allowed it?"

"His parents have multiple tattoos themselves. They encouraged him to do what he wanted, in every way. They are the most liberal parents I've ever heard about." She looked up. "Why do you ask?"

"I bet I could play Q and A with you for the next hour, and you'd know all the answers about Raiden." She squeezed Lesley's arm. "Don't you see? You *are* interested in him. And if he were a customer, you wouldn't sit on my couch crying your eyes out."

"Damn it. I hate feelings."

The collar was unlocked once the guard with the cell phone nodded toward his colleague that he was done. Raiden felt misused, even when he was allowed to put on a pair of shorts the second guard provided. His own clothes were gone. He hadn't noticed who had taken them. It didn't matter anymore. He couldn't think about anything else but how to run away from this dreadful place.

"What will you do with that video and the pictures?"

"Shut your face, shithead. You don't ask no questions." The guard used the handcuffs again. "Open your mouth one more time, and I'll push you into the black box for another twelve hours. Do you want that?"

Raiden lowered his chin. Though many questions burned in him, he wouldn't risk what little freedom he'd been granted. He turned his hands in the cuffs. He was at the mercy of the guards, and they loved what they were doing. He had seen it all before—the power-hungry bastards who lived it up while spreading misery everywhere. Keeping victims small and helpless gave them a hard-on. Being restricted guaranteed those men power over everyone. Raiden was disgusted but also in deep fear.

"Fine." The guard pushed him along the corridor, then turned to his companion. "What about his collar? Do you have it?"

"There's none left." The second man huffed. "Too many newcomers."

Raiden walked past cells with men with buzz cuts, stubble, and wearing nothing else on their bodies than boxer shorts and muscle shirts. They looked like hardened survivors. Some had scars, bruises, and several featured barely healed cuts above eyebrows and cheekbones. They observed Raiden with skeptical interest. Raiden sensed their curiosity and also their rejection. He felt like a yacht among smaller vessels, an exotic and rarely seen appearance that was admired but also rejected and envied. One of the men spat on the ground as if uttering a silent challenge.

The guard put a hand on his shoulder to make Raiden walk faster until they reached an empty cell. The handcuffs came off, and the guard stepped out with the distinct order that he'd be back in the black hole if he made trouble. The guard slammed the door hard enough that Raiden jerked.

Fear of being locked up for good cut off his breath. When the key was turned in the lock, he felt as though he was underwater trying to surface. Someone was keeping him down, and he knew he would drown. His heart pounded hard and fast, making him dizzy.

Raiden had suffered a near-death experience when he was nineteen. His scuba tank had jammed between two rocks, and he'd had been unable to pull it out. After taking one last breath, he had slipped out of the straps and begun to ascend as slowly as he could, fearing that if he surfaced too fast, he'd suffer from decompression. Though he saw the sunlight, he held his breath and his speed until he broke through, breathless and on the brink of unconsciousness. The day at sea had taught him that recklessness — in this case diving alone and without knowing the sea bottom — was the perfect way to suicide.

Right now, Raiden felt like he was caught close to the bottom without a chance to rise toward the sun. The steel around him was more dangerous than the rocks. He couldn't escape with a clever maneuver and discipline. The walls appeared to narrow on him. If he couldn't find a way out, he'd die.

"Breathe," the man in the adjacent cell said quietly. "It's bad and oppressive to be imprisoned, but the walls won't kill you."

Raiden put his hands on his knees. Still, his heart hammered against his ribcage, while white dots danced before his eyes. He wanted to yell at someone to let him out but couldn't form a single word.

"Sit down and drink water. Calm down. You can't change

anything right now."

Another cell, but this time with a view. Raiden heeded the man's advice. When he felt better, he rubbed his painful wrists and dared to lift his gaze to the man's face in the adjacent cell. Like the other inmates, he looked strong, was in good shape, and bore signs of maltreatment. His left arm was bandaged, his knuckles crusted with dried blood. Raiden noticed that the man was older than the others by at least five years.

"I'm Tom," the man said with a small but friendly smile. "And you are?"

"Raiden." He had a hundred questions, but the most pressing were, "Do you have any idea why we're here? Why I was kidnapped?" He looked around. "What's happening at this place?"

Tom's lips curled into another sad smile. "Welcome to an illegal fight club with volunteers and others."

Nicolas had barely made it on time to the suit fitting, but his best friend was happy. There were jokes and friendly banter with the groom, and when the fitter was satisfied with their choices, Jason invited his best man and his friends to a nearby bar. On the way to their cars, Nicolas got a phone call from Agent Lawry to meet him at the office.

"This sounds like you're already married to her," Jason said, sounding like a jealous wife himself. "She calls you and you jump?" He shook his head and pretended to be disgusted. "I expected more from you."

"She's the agent leading the investigation. If she's got something that leads to finding Thomas, I'll meet her at the office whenever she wants."

"Oh, dear, that doesn't sound like Jacklyn should hear this."

Nicolas rolled his eyes, praying for equanimity. "If you don't tell her, I won't. I'll text her that I'll be late. Lesley's with her and needs all the comfort Jacky can give."

Jason's exuberant mood ebbed away. "So, there's been another kidnapping? One of Lesley's . . . friends?"

"Raiden is one of her frequent clients — so she says. Judging by her sorrow, he's much more, but she doesn't see that yet."

"What are the chances of finding Thomas and Raiden?" Jason's friends called for him to come over, and he sighed. "Are there chances at all?"

"They were kidnapped for a reason, so, yes I assume they're still alive."

"Best of luck." Jason patted Nicolas's shoulder. "Thank you all the more for taking the time tonight. See you at the office . . .later."

Christina introduced Nicolas to Jacques Arpin, a slender man with black hair, a small mustache, and black-framed glasses which he adjusted repeatedly during his monologue about the Darknet, a system behind the global internet and more difficult to access than the vaults in big banks. Arpin explained that the Darknet had been developed in the seventies and was a kind of parallel network to the overall known internet, either encrypted or running on a specific protocol that allowed users — and that meant insiders — to connect to it. The Darknet hosted drug dealers as well as weapons dealers and criminals who sold pornography — either on video or with a link to prostitution rings that delivered men and women to wealthy customers. The FBI as well as the NSA tried to infiltrate the Darknet to crack down those criminals, but despite some hits on major dealers, the platforms prospered. If one was closed, another one opened a few weeks later. Additionally, the FBI was underfunded and needed more qualified agents to keep up with the criminals.

"It's a fight against windmills." Arpin shrugged. "But you aren't here for a history lesson or my current problems of how to keep track on high-profile gangsters." He opened a site with lots of pictures, all of them X-rated. "These photographs belong to a site selling male fighters, more the Roman style than . . ."

Nicolas's mouth was dry. He took a deep breath, bracing for the bad news.

Arpin turned around to look at him skeptically. "If this is not your cup of tea, I can close the site and tell you what I found."

"I'll make it."

Arpin twitched his brows, but then went on, adjusting his glasses. "We're constantly running facial recognition programs over these sites. We search missing persons, kidnap victims, runaways. The programs reach their limits once the parameters can't be met, for example when the person has a lot of hair hanging across her or his face, or when the picture wasn't taken full frontal but at a slant of more than twenty degrees or a profile. Here, the gangsters used black stripes across their victims' eyes. The program's unable to compare the remaining matches and comes up with nil."

He scrolled through a series of pictures showing faces and naked bodies. Nicolas had a notion he wouldn't like what Arpin was about to tell him. Arpin stopped at a series of pictures with the same details and pointed at the man's chin.

"Here, you see a scar the stubble doesn't cover. It must've been a deep wound once. The program didn't see a resemblance, but I did. And I compared the other details I had." Arpin looked at Nicolas. "It's your friend Thomas."

Nicolas's breath caught in his throat. Even if he wanted to, he couldn't say a word. He was horrified by the revelation that his friend was displayed on an illegal website selling men like merchandise. Christina patted his shoulder and set a glass of water on the table in front of him.

Arpin scrolled the pictures back and forth, showing Thomas's front and backside. All pictures were taken in a tiled area, looking like a bathroom. "Though I identified your friend by the scar, I can't tell you the origin of the pictures, where they were uploaded, and who runs the website. I can't tell you where it's based. I'm still digging deeper, but the firewall is one of a kind. As soon as I know more, I'll let you know."

"What about Raiden?" Nicolas's voice was hoarse. He cleared his throat to repeat the question. "Did you find him, too?"

"I ran his description. He's a unique guy. If they didn't alter his appearance too much — short hair, no beard, make-up for the tattoos — either the program or I will find him. Do you think he'll show up here?"

"We assume he was kidnapped by the same paramilitary men," Christina said in her clear and friendly voice. "It's a good guess that he'll show up, too. And the word *unique* describes him best. Raiden Stroud cannot be missed."

Chapter Eight

"You're saying you were kidnapped but Miguel wasn't?" Raiden's head seemed to spin faster with every minute. Though he was still hungry, the revelations suppressed his appetite. "He wanted to fight, but you were brought here against your will. Well, that's my fate, too." Raiden pushed his long hair back. "The men overwhelmed me at the parking lot and dragged me into a van." He looked around. "Do the fights take place daily?"

"No, that's just sparring." Tom changed his position on the cot, grimacing when he rested his bandaged arm on his thigh. "The boss of this operation, a man called *the Player*, arranges the fights. You'll recognize him when you see him. His face is marred by scars, and he exudes a wave of authority. The fights are a big deal. Lots of people in the audience."

"He's different," Miguel mumbled, nodding with his chin at Raiden.

Raiden frowned. "Why am I different?"

"Look around." Miguel bared his yellow teeth. "You still have your long hair, your beard. We lost it to the clippers." He ran a hand across his scalp. "I had wonderful hair. It's all gone now. And the guards see that it stays that way."

Raiden swallowed. The fear that had abated once the guards had taken him to a cell instead of locking him up in the black hole returned with the same intensity. "You're saying I'm meant for something other than fighting?"

"Could be." Miguel made a face. "Who knows?"

Raiden held tight to the bars toward Tom's cell, looking

straight at Miguel. "Do you know why I was kidnapped? Do you know anything? Tell me!"

Miguel made a dismissive gesture, then glanced at Tom. "No one says a word here. The guards are brutal. They beat you, they're cruel, and they don't hesitate to give you a thrashing if they want. But they don't talk. No one says a word about what's going on here." He shrugged. "You learn from what you see. You observe, but questions are useless."

Raiden rested his arms against the cold steel and hung his head. "What the hell do they want from me?"

Nicolas left the glass of water untouched but fled the room the moment Arpin finished his presentation. He made it to a stall at the men's room and threw up what he had eaten. The picture of Thomas being advertised for sale was burned into his mind. He would never forget what he had seen. His friend was on the market for a bunch of sickos who spent thousands of dollars on their criminal operations.

His mind spun the idea further until Nicolas stood at the sink, holding tight to the rim, panting with exhaustion and sorrow that he couldn't do more than hope that the FBI would find him. If Thomas were sold to some crazy shithead, the FBI and the ATF would face a hard and probably fruitless investigation. He couldn't stand the thought that his friend might be taken out of reach.

He washed his hands and face and left the men's room to find Christina waiting for him.

"Are you feeling better?"

"Not really. If there's nothing else tonight, I'll drive home."

"Maybe tomorrow you can tell me why you know Miss Gilbert." Her smile indicated she wanted to cheer him up, but he wasn't in the mood.

"Maybe." He shuffled to his car, trying to decide whether

he would tell Jacklyn about Thomas's fate or not.

Raiden couldn't stop trembling. It was bad enough he was locked up. It was worse to learn that it was possible he had to fight one of the men in the adjacent cells. They looked hard and experienced — men who knew how to fight. Raiden had had his share of brawls, but back in his teenage years, his size and his impressive demeanor combined with his strength had been enough to cow competitors. Raiden's parents had taught him to use his brain instead of his biceps, in spite of his well-trained body. Raiden used to discuss problems, not batter his opponent. Following his parents' advice, he had learned swimming, diving, sailing a boat. If he were to face one of the men he saw, he knew he'd drop unconscious in the first round and not get up again.

Brutally honest, the Mexican with the heavy accent had described how the fights took place and that there were no rules. Raiden panicked at the thought that any of the men would raise his fists against him in such a gladiator fight. When Miguel added that many times the loser was pulled out of the ring to never return, Raiden wanted to press his body through the bars and run away as fast as he could.

To calm his mind and since there was nothing else to do, he drank water and looked at Tom, who sat on the cot observing him.

"How can you stay so cool?" Raiden asked. He wrung his hands endlessly and paced up and down the small cell without getting anywhere. "I can't stop thinking that I'll die here at the hands of a stranger because I was abducted by a bunch of his cronies who didn't give me a clue why they took me."

"I know that one of my enemies chose me to die in the first fight," Tom said in a flat voice. He lifted and dropped his hand. "And I'm not cool. *On this highway, the roadkill is human.*

I'm trying not to panic that my next opponent will smash my face. I blindsided the first one, but that won't happen again."

"I'm not a fighter. I put my hopes in my girlfriend," Raiden said, sitting down. He ran a hand through his hair. "She knows that I was kidnapped. She'll try to find me."

"She's with the police?"

"No. She's . . . She knows someone working for the FBI in DC. He's a cool guy—looks like a Nordic athlete—and he'll do what he can. I bet they're already brooding over a strategy how to find out where I am."

"DC you said?" Thomas asked with sudden interest. "Who are you talking about?"

Raiden hesitated and broke eye contact. No one was his friend in here. He shouldn't be gullible enough to believe that Thomas was an exception because he acted like someone who cared. Every forced fighter would do what he could to get out of this prison.

Thomas cast him an encouraging glance. "I'm just asking because I know someone who's with the FBI. Nick and I had a mission together. Since then, we've been friends."

"Nick?" Raiden bent forward, his arms on his thighs. "Are you talking about Nicolas Hayes?"

The Player reclined in his favorite chair, a glass of bourbon in one hand, a cigar in the other. He had smoked cigarettes in his younger years but preferred the taste of a good cigar now. Such delicacies were restricted to special evenings. He had closed another very fortunate deal, and Kevin and his chosen men had fulfilled the contract for the kidnapping perfectly. The Player simpered into the darkness. The young man he had ordered to be his toy that night had been more than giving. In his gratitude, the Player had sent him away with a sizeable tip. Looking at the entangled sheets on the bed, he couldn't be more contented.

When the telephone rang, he thought about ignoring it and sighed when he recognized the number.

"Mr. Cheng wants to know whether you were able to obtain his merchandise," the Chinese man with the heavy accent said.

The Player sat up straight in his chair and put down the cigar. "I was."

"Good. When will you deliver the merchandise to a location you are free to name?"

"The merchandise will be on display at the night's entertainment a few days ahead."

Silence on the line.

The Player simpered, knowing he had shocked Mr. Cheng. He sipped bourbon and smoked while he waited. He had never met Mr. Cheng in person, only his assistant, a man with thick glasses who called himself Mr. Wong. The Player knew that Mr. Wong had special sexual interests himself but didn't dare utter them. The Player wondered if Mr. Cheng shared the merchandise he bought with his willing helper.

"This was not the agreement," Mr. Wong said, stressing every word. "The agreement was—"

"You asked me whether he could use my service to acquire an object he desired. I sent my men to DC, and they brought back the merchandise, as requested. The agreement didn't include that he'd be delivered to your doorstep."

Once more, stunned silence ensued, and the Player wondered whether to empty the glass and refill it or savor the last sip until after the call. He was about to lift the glass when Mr. Wong spoke again, as accentuated as before but with the undertone of fury.

"Mr. Cheng is very dissatisfied. He assumed he had made himself clear that he wanted to receive the object right after you had acquired it. The money was already deposited in the account you named."

"Correct. Thank you. It'll be considered your first bid at the auction."

"Auction? There will be another one?"

The Player's lips curled to a smile. He knew how to convince his clients to return to the gambling table. "Yes. I'll let you know the time and date shortly."

"Thank you. Mr. Cheng says that negotiating with you is harder than building the Great Wall."

"I take that as a compliment. Good night."

The Player stood up to refill his glass.

Thomas's eyes widened. "You know Nick?"

Raiden lowered his chin, chuckling. Suddenly, his ribcage didn't seem as constricted. He leaned against the wall. "Yes, yes, I know him. We met ten days ago at his place for breakfast."

"Ten days." Thomas's face fell. "I was kidnapped eleven days ago."

"Oh, I'm sorry." Raiden's spark of optimism died. "You've survived here for eleven days. That's . . . an accomplishment, under the circumstances."

"So, you're friends with Nick?"

"Not quite. My mistress and Jacklyn are best friends."

"The lady with the dungeon." Thomas frowned, opened his mouth and closed it again.

"If you assume Lesley's my girlfriend, you're right. She's my mistress *and* my girlfriend."

"I see. Quite a catch—from what I heard about her. Nick's not talkative when it comes to those aspects of his relationship with Jacklyn. He told me that he'd been to the dungeon of Jacklyn's friend—whether for business or for fun, he didn't say."

Raiden read Thomas's expression like an open book. He accepted Nick's sexual orientation without understanding it and without striving to learn more about it. Raiden assumed Thomas was a man living a happy life with a lovely woman, all sweet and romantic.

"Lesley's a fantastic woman. I was surprised and happy that she let me join in for breakfast with her friends."

"If you're her lover — why should she not?"

Raiden searched for words to explain the situation, but Thomas dismissed the question with a wave of his hand.

"It doesn't matter. Fact is, Nick will do everything in his power to speed the investigation. The FBI has its own division for kidnapping cases. Once they're on track, they'll find us."

Raiden felt a surge of hope, then lowered his voice confidentially. "Do you know why they took pictures and a video of me under the shower? Did they do that with you, too?"

"Yes, they did. I have no idea. Miguel's right — the guards don't talk. You can only learn from what you see."

"And I stand out," Raiden stated and pointed along the row of fighters. "What the hell am I doing here?"

Three days later, the Player had a private meeting with a much-appreciated partner, the agriculture commissioner Lawrence Stone. In a separate room at his favorite restaurant, he welcomed his guest with a handshake and a smile and told him that he had ordered his favorite appetizer, clam chowder.

Stone laughed a deep belly laugh and waved a finger at him. "Ah, you're trying to charm me with a treat! Marvelous! But, yes, I admit I'm a *connoisseur*."

They sat down.

The Player kept smiling but thought that a whale like Stone needed a radical diet — no fat meat, no cholesterol, and lots of rigorous exercise. "I know." He waited until their drinks were served, then went on. "As you know, my company will throw a little party the day after tomorrow. I'd be delighted if you could join us."

Stone's Adam's apple jumped. His eyes as well as his nostrils widened, and his gaze was intense. He blushed so heavily that his round head seemed close to exploding. The Player read anticipation and hunger.

Stone played with the napkin on the table as he tried to get a grip on his emotions. "You know that I've got a tight schedule."

"I know. Still, I had hoped that — given notice ahead — you might want to attend the event, even for a short time."

Stone wet his lips and changed position on the chair. His breathing accelerated. "The same place?"

"Yes." The Player maintained a business smile. "I assure you that you won't regret your appearance."

Stone emptied his glass and signaled the waitress he wanted another drink. He blotted his forehead with the crumpled napkin. His voice rose a notch. "Will there be . . . merchandise to buy?"

"And entertainment and bets, as you already know." The Player turned on his most amiable smile. He didn't believe his luck that one of the most influential politicians wasn't just a connoisseur of good American food, but also of young men in their prime, preferably looking like *Hercules*. When the Player first discovered Stone's preferences, he had put him under surveillance for a month and found out about a secluded cottage and the young men Stone invited there to fulfill his sexual desire. At first, the Player had pondered blackmailing Stone. In the conversation, however, Stone had not only confessed his deeds but asked the Player whether it was at all possible to provide him with young men he could treat like servants — outstanding payment was no problem. He claimed it would make a dream come true.

The Player was used to hiding his astonishment, and he had hidden it well. Within an hour, Stone had agreed to help the Player with his growing venture by declaring it an official factory for the packing industry. If the Player used one part of the compound for agricultural products and packing, Stone had explained, it was easy to justify the many transport vehicles and the men working on the fields. The men had parted as business partners looking forward to a prospering enterprise.

"I admit I don't like to be seen by so many other clients," Stone said, making a face. He loosened his tie and opened the first button of his dress shirt. "I'm uncomfortable that others are in the know."

"Believe me, Lawrence, my other clients say the same. No one will give you away. They know that I could either uncover dirty secrets or have them killed within an hour." He simpered. "We're all on safe ground. That being said — can I put you on the guest list?"

"Oh, yes." Stone sipped his drink and grinned like a fool when the steaming soup was served. "Put me on the list."

Nicolas sat down on the chair at Christina's desk and declined the coffee she offered. "What did you find out?"

Christina raised her perfectly plucked brows. "It's not progressing any faster with you rapping on my door every day."

"What did you find out?"

She poured coffee and sat down at her computer. Gaze fixed on the screen, she frowned and pressed her lips tight. Her voice was void of emotion. "The Chinese man we watched on the video calls himself Mr. Wong. I'm certain it's a false name but a good one. The passport is valid, and we couldn't find any flaws. But then, Wong is one of the most frequent names in China. The day we watched him at the dungeon, he called a company named *Fine Goods Consolidated.* They deal with artifacts, jewelry, and works of art. The company actually exists and exchanges goods with the US and China regularly." She looked at Nicolas. "Mr. Wong called the company's DC office, but it's unclear who he talked to. It's clear, though, that Mr. Wong is an employee with an apartment in the suburbs. We checked it—nothing out of the ordinary."

"If he has anything to do with the kidnappings—was it wise to search his home?"

"He doesn't know we were there. We placed bugs, took a look around, and left without a trace. If he picks up the phone again, we'll know and monitor him."

"Hmm." Nicolas sensed a flaw in the investigation but couldn't name it. "Anything about the destination of the kidnapping victims?"

"Based on the description Mrs. Freeman delivered, the police and the FBI check every gray van they see. Don't roll your eyes. Yesterday, the police stopped a gray van—they didn't find the kidnappers, rather a group of four men with equipment for their next break-in. It's not that we're sitting on our asses, Nicolas."

"I didn't say that." He got up and paced the room. "Since I saw what the gangsters plan with Tom, I can't stop thinking that we're too slow, too late. Right now, he might be at a location we can find, somehow. Once he's . . . sold, there's no chance anymore to get to him. The same goes for the other victims. Did Raiden's pictures show up, too?"

"No. We're checking the Chinese company. If Mr. Wong has anything to do with the kidnapping, we'll know that soon enough. But we have to do this by the book, or the judge won't accept any evidence at court. You know that."

Nicolas put his hands in his pants pockets and lowered his chin.

"I know this case carries a lot of personal feelings." Christina's voice was soothing. "You know two of the victims, and that's why Sullivan didn't let you join. I don't mind you staying, but your presence doesn't speed our work in any way."

"I get it. You don't want me here." He turned to leave.

"Nicolas, don't get this wrong, but Sullivan didn't grant you authorization to work with us. He's got his reasons, and they're sound. I will keep you in the loop, as promised."

"Are you going to interrogate Mr. Wong?"

Christina made a face. "We tried but couldn't find him. Though he's an official employee, the company's secretary told us that he's constantly traveling and doesn't show up at the office daily. We left our invitation and put out a BOLO."

"I doubt that you'll find him." Nicolas tried and failed to smile. "But thanks for trying."

"One more thing. The Virginia State Police told us this morning they're closing in on one of the suspects of the Turner family who escaped the police during the raid. They promised to hand him over once they found him."

"It's not Tyrone, right?"

"No, but it could be that this man has information about him."

It was late afternoon when Thomas was taken back to his cell. He could tolerate hunger and thirst for a while, but the overbearing weariness and the pain that came with it was more than he could take. Groaning, he sat on the cot and carefully touched his ribs. The training got harder every day. His impression that the sparring was meant to keep him in shape and try some moves was obviously wrong. Under the influence of *Tyrone the Butcher*, the training had evolved into a brutal slugfest without a chance to quit. Thomas had a ringing in his ears from a hard blow to the side of his head. Tyrone had watched the fight with growing agitation, and then—to Thomas's surprise—a guard he hadn't seen so far called for the fight to stop. Without an explanation, Thomas had been ordered to return to his cell.

Whoever had called the shots, he was grateful he could sit down and nurse his injuries.

Behind him, Raiden got up. "How are you?"

"Bad and getting worse." Thomas got up to fetch a cup of water and the plate with food. Every move was an ordeal. "If it's going to keep on like this, I won't make it to the next official fight. If anything around here can be called *official*." He looked at the young man. "Any news? Did you hear about the next fight? When it will take place?"

"Rumor has it it'll take place the day after tomorrow. It's from someone at the packing station."

Thomas frowned. "What are you doing there?"

Raiden pushed back his hair. He looked sweaty and worn out, his eyes hollow. "The guards take me to the next wing. It's like walking into another . . . realm. Totally different from this prison block. There's a kind of factory. Many workers, tons of canned food. My job is to pack the cans in boxes for shipping."

Thomas stopped chewing. "Any chance to get away from there undetected?"

Raiden's laugh was more like a sob. "None. The guards are everywhere, and we have chains around our waists, connected to a ring in the floor. I can sit down or stand, but I can't leave my position."

"Cruel bastards. What did you see?"

"The land around the buildings must be vast. I saw workers and more guards." He huffed. "We're in the middle of nowhere and don't even know what state we're being kept in."

"Did you see trucks?"

"Yes, but I couldn't read the license plates, and the drivers don't come close. They don't know who we are and that we're held against our will. If anyone dares to shout, he's taken away." He trembled visibly. "They've got methods to cow the men. I bet the black hole is just one of them. The people are trembling with fear and don't raise their heads." Raiden twitched his brows as he rested his forearms on the bars. Though the prisoners received enough food, he appeared to have lost weight. "Are you thinking about home? I bet you have a wonderful wife waiting for you."

"How did you know her? Should I be jealous?"

"I can see in your eyes that you're in love and can't wait to see her again."

Thomas sighed. He wished for nothing more than to hold his wife in his arms again. "You're right. Charlene's a wonderful woman. She's expecting our first child." His heart wanted to explode with emotion, so he paused until he trusted his voice again. "I'll be a father in three months."

"Wow. That's a good reason to bear this and survive."

"But to do this we have to find out more about our captors and where we are. We need details, routines. So far, the guards show up in irregular intervals, don't have a strict routine, and there are so many of them, no man comes up here twice. There's no way we can try to get them on our side." Thomas shook his head. He had mulled over their chances to escape so often, he was devastated. The prison was perfect. The human factor consisted of trained men who were obviously well paid and resilient to any kind of bribery. They had no morals and did what they were told. He saw glee in their eyes when they maltreated the prisoners. Those men wouldn't act in the name of mercy.

"If we want to get away, we have to use force." Thomas looked up to meet Raiden's skeptical gaze. "Yes, I know, you're no fighter, but I don't see any other way. I have to overwhelm one of them, grab his weapon and take the fight to the next one. If I can free the others, they'll help. As I see it, about half the men have been forced to fight."

Raiden shook his head. "This plan works if the guards aren't allowed to shoot you."

"They don't carry guns. Taser weapons and cudgels."

"And cattle prods. They aren't picky and use them as they please." Raiden grunted. "Your plan depends on you over-whelming a guard. Right now, you don't look as if you'd fight the next few days."

"They will let me fight," Thomas replied with conviction. "Tyrone, that bastard, made sure that I'm not in my best shape. He hopes my opponent will strike me down in the first round."

"Why doesn't he fight you?"

"Because he's an asshole and a coward. He only fights when he knows he can win—against women and chained enemies."

"You two have a history?"

"Oh, yes." Thomas finished eating and put down the plate before he lay down on his cot to recap his undercover job in Florence Town and the final arrest of most of the Turner family members. "Jebediah and Tyrone came to my friend's home and wanted to kill me. Instead, I shot Jebediah in the shoulder. He was arrested and put to trial. Tyrone escaped and was clever enough to stay out of sight."

"The grudge he bears is bigger than an ocean liner."

"You bet." Thomas closed his eyes. "He won't stop pestering me until I kill him."

"You think you can do this?"

"It's him or me."

Nicolas opened the door, and both Jacklyn and Lesley got up from the couch to welcome him, their eyes filled with fear.

"Any news?"

Nicolas shook his head. He thought of several evenings when he had come home to find Jacklyn and Lesley dressed up in leather and lace, ready to play with him. It was odd to see them in jogging pants and t-shirts, especially Lesley, who appeared to have no other apparel than black leather in all its varieties.

He summed up what Christina had told him but left out what Arpin had shown him on the Darknet. No matter which fate the other kidnapping victims faced, Nicolas was convinced that Raiden would be sold. Given his history and sexual preferences, he was a candidate for every kind of games in every kind of bedroom.

"We should look at it positively," Jacklyn said as she went into the kitchen. "Unless a body shows up, we can assume Raiden is alive."

Nicolas sat down opposite Lesley, refraining from correcting Jacklyn that the police had found no bodies so far. He was tired from the day's events and his work. Jason and he had a new case, and Nicolas was torn between two equally important tasks. "I was astonished at the list of clients your business serves."

Lesley's small smile was replaced by sadness. "Trying to distract me from my misery? Very well. Yes, my list is growing. But that's happening because Harry Fuller modified his business. *Club Destiny* is no longer an erotic club with a dungeon, but a nightclub for singers, songwriters, and classy dancers. He's out of the erotic niche. That means I've got more possibilities and a wider range of clients. Some of the local politicians choose my club now."

"That's interesting. Did Harry give a reason?"

Lesley shrugged. "He claims that Jacky had the idea."

Jacklyn turned at the stove. "Oh, had I?"

"I'm happy to serve the needs of those men. As long as they

come to clubs like mine, they don't expect their lovers or wives to do this at home."

Nicolas's eyebrows went up as his eyes widened. "Their wives?"

"Sure. I know of happy couples who live a wonderful life together, but she either can't or won't serve her husband's needs. Therefore, he comes to me — his wife knows that — and he walks home after the session. Both are happy with that solution." Lesley touched Nicolas's cheek, a gentle gesture so unlike the Lesley he knew. "Love comes in so many varieties, we should never take anything for granted or dismiss it as crazy."

"I'm the last one to call sexual preferences *crazy*." When Lesley pursed her lips, he continued, "It's not what I like or dislike, but I have to keep a professional attitude. I don't mind any sex game as long as both partners agree." He glanced at Jacklyn, who bowed to him in mock gratitude.

Lesley got up. "I should drive to my club, see what's going on."

"We won't let you go without dinner."

"But I have to—"

Out of impulse, Nicolas took her in his arms and held her as she started crying.

"Tell me about your wife. How did you two meet?"

Thomas kept his eyes closed. He was too weary to look up, and there was nothing to see but the bars and the corridor where a guard walked by, checking the inmates. Downstairs, another sparring was taking place. He heard hammering fists and grunted curses.

"Charlene worked at the diner in the small town where I was sent to investigate undercover. The ATF assumed the Turners were building bombs, and we wanted to know about their intentions." Thomas sighed. The memory of his first night with Charlene was sweet. "Charlene and I fell in love so quickly, it was amazing. Her father didn't want me around — I was an outsider, not a son born in town. And yet she stayed by my side."

Raiden hummed with content. "That's rare."

"Yes, it is." Thomas glanced at the much younger man. "Charlene and I made plans to leave town, but she couldn't wait until my assignment was done. So I took her to the bus station, but I remained behind."

"To investigate?"

"Yes. She made it to Richmond, where a friend of mine fetched her and took her home." Once more, he opened his eyes.

Raiden stared at him, obviously captivated by this story.

"Unfortunately, her wannabe lover was in league with the sheriff's son and they . . ." Thomas took a deep breath. "They were not amused."

"I bet."

"After the arrest of some criminal members of the Turner family and others, who had committed ever more severe crimes, Charlene and I searched for a house and moved in. I'd never been happier in my life. She was so exuberant that we moved in together she was stumbling over her feet. We didn't have much money, but friends donated a lot of stuff. She couldn't believe their generosity. She became a talented interior designer within a week. When I think of her, I think of a bed of flowers that looks bleary in winter but overwhelmingly beautiful in spring. That's Charlene. Now that she's pregnant it's even better. She's looking forward to being a mom, and she's constantly talking about the baby and that she'll sew him clothes. She even asked a neighbor to teach her knitting." Thomas stopped when emotion got the best of him. "She'll be a wonderful mom."

"Yes, she's a caring woman, and she makes you happy. That's the best part of it."

Thomas forced a smile even though he felt like breaking down inside. "Once we're out of this shithole, I'll introduce you."

"That'd be great."

"You can bring your mistress, if she leaves the floggers at home."

Raiden laughed. "Oh, I think I can arrange that."

CHAPTER NINE

The Player looked from Arturo to Juan and back. He had come to know both men as reliable business partners. They had their flaws, preferences, habits, but none of those had ever influenced their effectiveness or reliability. However, the idiotic sidekick named Tyrone altered the Player's appraisal.

"I can't put my disappointment in words you'd understand." The Player exhaled, watching both men belligerently. "I run a business here. You added a fighter to the club, and now your . . . *buddy* goads the other fighters to knock him out! That's not the intention of the sparring. Do you understand that? Is your pal able to understand that? You can tell him that he must stay away from my fighters, or I'll throw him out. Is that clear enough for you?"

"What's the big deal?" Juan asked, shrugging and opening his arms. His English bore a heavy Mexican accent. "He'll be fodder for the next fighter anyway."

The Player lifted his chin and straightened to his full height, staring at the men on the other side of his desk. "I was very lenient, almost compliant to your buddy. You didn't tell me that Thomas works for the ATF. You left me in the dark concerning the risks of the investigation that has ensued. I had Thomas kidnapped because your buddy wanted him here. But what happens with a fighter is my decision and my decision alone."

"He can still fight," Arturo said, equally disinterested. He adjusted the sunglasses on his greased hair and looked smug.

"And it was the plan from the beginning that he'd be a bonus, right?"

"His kidnapping cost the same time and effort as kidnapping any other man I had on the list. But this one wouldn't have been my preferred choice. In any case, you and this guy, Tyrone, stay away from my fighters. Any other violation—"

"All right, we got it." Juan took a cigarette from behind his ear and lit it. He sounded bored. "The fighters are your business, and we'll let Ty know that Thomas is off limits. Will that do? We've brought you fighters all along, so why are you making a fuss?" When the Player was about to contradict him, Juan lifted a hand. "Yeah, yeah, keep your cool. We must go. We've got other things . . ." He made a gesture. "You know."

The Player dismissed them with a wave of his hand and sat behind his desk again. He had distrusted the babbling youngster from the beginning, but obviously not even Kevin had been able to keep the idiot from doing mischief. When he had seen Thomas sparring against one of the hardened men, he had been terrified by the intensity of the fight. After Thomas had hit the floor the first time, the Player identified Tyrone on the other side of the arena and immediately ordered the fight to end. Judging by the looks of it, Thomas had lived through several intense rounds. It was a shame. After his surprising victory, the bets had gone through the roof. Injured and slow, he would lose in the first round of the next fight and thus trigger suspicion that the fights were manipulated. The Player had sent the doctor to his cell to treat the wounds, but he wasn't optimistic. Cursing, he wished he had never let Tyrone enter the premises.

Christina sounded tired and disappointed on the phone. "We couldn't find out who Mr. Wong contacted. The *Fine Goods*

Consolidated is a group of companies owned by a Chinese mogul whose name is a mystery. We assume he's protected by the Chinese government and therefore untouchable."

"What about Mr. Cheng?" Nicolas asked. He was driving to a crime scene, and Jason beside him pointed to the highway exit. "Did you find him, at least?"

"No. It seems he learned of our investigation and preferred to leave the state. It's a dead end."

Nicolas steered the car toward the next intersection, cursing wordlessly.

"While this is bad news, I've got good news, too. We caught Brian Forrest, a friend of the Turners. My team threatened him hard enough that he revealed that Tyrone Turner left DC right after the hit on Thomas, heading for Mexico. Brian confessed he wanted to join him, but Tyrone claimed he had special ties with two guys named Juan and Arturo, no last name. They were like brothers to him." Christina paused, as if expecting praise.

Nicolas remained quiet.

"All right, moving on. We asked the Mexican police for support and learned that the brothers—last name *Gallego*— are visiting the US. I don't know why the Mexican police found out about them leaving their country and didn't tell us right away, but that's another story. The officer I talked to told me that the Gallegos deal with workers and marijuana, mostly. They've got their hands in pretty much every dirty deal north of the border."

"Is there a chance to arrest them? Do the Mexican police know of their whereabouts? Do they know of their partners in the US?"

"Not exactly. I phoned our bureaus in the south and asked for support. They're on it."

Nicolas steered the car toward the assembly of patrol cars with blue lights on. "If we find the brothers—"

"We'll find Tyrone and Thomas. Yes, I hope that, too."

Thomas sat up on his cot, grimacing with pain. Though the doc had treated him, the injuries hampered his movement. He groaned and held his head. Tyrone's spite followed him, even while he slept. His nightmares consisted of a bunch of armored thugs with weapons larger than their arms out to maim him. All Thomas could do was run away, but he wasn't fast enough, and Tyrone's evil laughter echoed in his ears.

He fetched a cup of water and was astonished to find a plate filled with slices of meat, mashed potatoes, and sweet corn. He ate hungrily.

Half an hour later, Raiden was brought back to his cell, accompanied by a cloud of fragrance.

The guard locked him in. "If you ruin yourself, you bet I'll make you pay. You got that? Hey! *You got that?*"

"Yes." Raiden's voice was meek. He sat down and ran both hands through his obviously freshly washed and cut hair. Even the boxer shorts and the white t-shirt appeared to be new.

Thomas saw that the young man was trembling badly. "What happened?"

"If only I knew!" He looked up. The fear in his eyes was raw. "I thought they'd take me to shower, but after that they tied me up on a bench, trimmed my beard, and shaved my whole body. And I mean it—everywhere! It was awful."

"Did they cut your nails, too?"

"Yeah, mock me."

"It's a grim sense of humor, believe me."

Raiden reached for a cup of water and spilled half of it. "And to answer your question—yes, I'm perfectly groomed and smooth as a baby's butt. Did that ever happen to you?"

"Showered and shaved? Yes. But you smell like a perfumery."

Miguel cocked his head and wrinkled up his nose. "Pretty boy, huh?"

Raiden's look spoke of bottomless fear. "This isn't for the fights, right? Why did they do this to me?"

Thomas glowered at Miguel, hoping he'd get the message to keep his mouth shut. The Mexican complied, but his gaze spoke volumes. Raiden would live through a humiliating night, and Thomas couldn't do anything to prevent it. He hated his helplessness. He hated to leave the young man alone when four guards showed up with handcuffs attached to the long chain to collect the fighters for the night.

When Thomas's cell was unlocked, he looked at Raiden, searching for words of encouragement while his fear increased. "Don't forget—*A hero will rise.* No matter what, my friend, keep your head high and trust in your friends. They will find us. Good luck."

"You, too. See you later."

Thomas forced a smile. "Yeah. Later."

"Do you have a moment?" Christina asked on the phone.

Nicolas stared at the two bodies on the ground in the living room of a wealthy home in Temple Hills, Maryland, and thought about the victims' lives and whether they had seen their killer enter their home while they were watching TV. This was the third couple killed within two months, and Sullivan had dropped the file on Jason's desk with the usual order to solve the case immediately.

He rubbed the bridge of his nose and turned away from the busy CSU team. "Yeah, I've got a moment." Outside, the October air was cool and fresh after a brief rain shower an hour ago. He inhaled deeply and wished he were home. He longed to embrace Jacklyn, to sit on the porch, and to let go of the devastating thoughts that followed him throughout the day.

"While the interrogation of Brian Forrest wasn't enlightening, the FBI field office in Montgomery, Alabama, told me that the Gallego brothers were responsible for the transport of a busload of men on interstate eighty-five to Columbus, probably coming from Mexico. The agents stopped the bus, but the passengers had valid papers and claimed they were en route to a factory in Perry, Georgia. The FBI had no choice but to let them pass. When I asked about the men, the agent in charge told me they were young and in good shape, none of them older than thirty."

"You think they're forced laborers?"

"That's one possibility. The other one—they're fighters, just like you thought. I contacted my colleagues in Atlanta to have them check the factory, if there is any. And they'll look through the interstate video surveillance. Maybe the destination was a ruse and they're driving elsewhere."

"Thank you, Christina, that sounds . . . promising."

"You're welcome."

Thomas relaxed his muscles and calmed his breathing. In the arena, the audience chatted loudly, placed bets, and called out to the fighters. The air was warm, filled with smoke and the stench of sweat. Beyond the large beams directed at the center of the boxing ring, Thomas caught a glimpse of Tyrone, who stood accompanied by his Mexican friends in the first row, agitated as a mean child. He gave Thomas a thumbs down. Even though Thomas hadn't seen his opponent yet, he answered with a confident grin. Tyrone's reaction consisted of flaring nostrils and a gush of obscenities.

Thomas couldn't care less. He wished the idiot would die of a heart attack, best accompanied by all the other gawkers who had arrived with their beer and enjoyed the appetizers the waiters served. He wished them all a terrible, slow death, so that they might understand their wrongdoing, but mostly to make sure they could never abuse people again.

The referee announced the fighters and encouraged the guests to come closer. The second fighter entered the ring. Thomas looked at the blond guy from the cell adjacent to Miguel's. He appeared as the role model for all the fighters to copy. His broad chest was shaven smooth, his haircut as short as it would get, and he radiated experience and endurance. In a silent challenge, he boxed one bandaged fist against the other and looked confident, bordering on arrogant. He radiated the aura of a seasoned fighter who would take up any challenge thrown at him.

"And here comes Etienne!" the referee shouted. "A well-known fighter and winner of the last two matches. In the other corner, you see Thomas, the one-time-lucky winner of the first round at the last fight night. He shouldn't be underestimated. Place your bets!"

Etienne twitched his brows when the referee ordered them to come to the center of the ring. Thomas knew he had a chance, but he pretended he could hardly walk the few steps.

Raiden thought that the time to fetch him was long past when two guards arrived, opened his cell, and handed him a dress shirt and a pair of black dress pants on a hanger.

"Here! Dress up and step out. Quick!"

Raiden got up and took the hanger, irritated. Upon the guard's impatient glare, he put on shirt and pants. "No shoes?"

"Trying to mock me? Get out!"

Raiden buttoned the shirt and hesitated when he saw a pair of handcuffs in the guard's hands. It was a rigid construction with a large ring in its center. His voice was but a breath. "What do you want from me?"

The second guard slammed a cudgel against the bars. "Step out and don't make a fuss!"

Raiden's heart hammered against his ribcage. Two men with cudgels were hard to battle, but he thought he could do it. If he gave in, he was lost and wouldn't get any chance again. He pretended to be in pain and shuffled toward the open door. The second guard stepped back to grant him room. Raiden lashed out to the right, hit the man's face hard enough that he stumbled, then reached for the cudgel, simultaneously evading the other guard's attack. Raiden wrested the cudgel from the guard's hand, swiveled around and struck the first guard's left arm. Behind him, the second man called for help via intercom.

The guard in front of him stepped back, thus pulling Raiden with him toward the corridor. Raiden couldn't see the second guard and had no time to turn around while he exchanged blows with his opponent. He thought he was winning when he hit the man's stomach. He saw him double over and cough, then the other guard grabbed his chin from behind, kicked the back of his knee, and when Raiden went down with a cry of pain, pressed an injection into his neck.

"Fuck this asshole!" the first guard shouted, hands on his knees. He looked as if he wanted to smash Raiden's face, but instead he shook his head and wheezed like an old man.

Raiden heard his own labored breathing. His knees were weak, and the man's features blurred in front of him. The cudgel slipped from his numbing hands. "No, not again," he mumbled. "Bastards."

"You asked for it," the guard behind him said, panting. "You're in luck they want you for the parade. I know what I'd do otherwise with a piece of shit like you!"

Raiden's arms were drawn back and cuffed so that he

couldn't move his hands and arms anymore. He had enough experience to know that the pain would set in within thirty minutes.

"Open your mouth."

For as long as he could remember, Raiden had loved being gagged. He liked to run his tongue along the rubber or wood and enjoyed the domination over his ability to speak, accompanied by more cuffs restricting his movement.

This time, Raiden dreaded being muted. The gag was made of thin metal covered by transparent plastic, formed with a small tongue depressor in its center. The gag was stylish, slim, and yet effective. Once inserted, Raiden couldn't use his tongue anymore and wouldn't form any understandable word. The guard fastened the *Velcro* at the back of his head but under the mass of hair. Last, the guard put a black hood over Raiden's head.

"Let's go!"

Etienne attacked Thomas right after the bell rang for the first round. Elegantly, Thomas avoided the hurried blows, danced around the ring, and kept his focus on his opponent to find weaknesses. Etienne knew how to box, but he clearly considered Thomas a loser he could easily smash. Thomas saw the hunger in the man's eyes. Whatever the reasons for his participation, Etienne was determined to hammer his adversary to the floor. Repeatedly, Etienne lashed out, but neither his jabs nor his punches were precise.

Toward the end of the round, Thomas recognized his chance when Etienne stood unbalanced and dropped his fists. It wasn't more than an inch, but enough for Thomas to jab his nose with all force he could muster. Etienne stumbled backward and tripped over his feet, crying out in pain. As he tried to regain his balance and pull up his defense, Thomas bridged the distance to knock him down with a direct hit to his chin. Etienne fell against the ropes but had no strength to hold on to them. He slipped to the floor, unconscious.

Thomas felt like dropping down beside him. He stumbled to his corner. His arms were taut like bowstrings and hurt like hell. Around him, the crowd cheered, and the referee announced the winner. When Thomas turned, Tyrone stood right next to the ring, out of control and spitting with rage. If he'd had the strength, Thomas would have laughed in his face.

"It's not over!" Tyrone yelled.

Thomas wished he could lift his middle finger in his direction.

After a twenty-minute ride in a van, Raiden was led into a warm room that smelled of flowers. It was quiet now that the cheering of the audience at the boxing ring was behind them. His captors stopped and turned him to the side. The tight shackles were connected with a chain to a metal column behind him. The guard locked a collar around his neck. The hood came off, and Raiden took a shaky breath as he looked around. He couldn't have been more flabbergasted by the sight of a spaceship.

The guard knelt in front of him to spread his legs and lock his ankles in a leg spreader. Even though he was dressed, Raiden felt terrible—helpless, vulnerable. This was no prelude to a session with sexual connotation, where a mistress would approach and seduce him. He was breathless to realize that he was being displayed like merchandise in a large and stylish showroom with paintings along the walls and five rows of rose-colored armchairs. Six shackled men—dressed like him—were lined up at the wall, illuminated by large overhead spotlights. They were young and attractive, tall, and muscular. The men were eye-catchers every model agency would hire on the spot.

The man next to Raiden whimpered as tears trickled down his cheeks. His long black hair and bronze skin identified him as Native American. Like the other victims, he had exotic looks that attracted men and women likewise. He looked as terrified as Raiden felt.

Raiden tried to see the others when a guard stood at his side to brush his hair and wipe his face with a wet tissue. After that, he combed Raiden's beard again. Raiden tried to move his head, but the chain connecting his collar to the column behind him was too short.

Once finished, all the guards stood back against the wall, silent watchers to the show that would soon begin.

CHAPTER TEN

Thomas heard the referee call his name and dropped the water bottle he was holding. "Me? Again?" He couldn't believe his ears and was dumbfounded that the guard pointed at him to leave the cage.

"Good luck," Miguel mumbled beside him.

"Not this time." Thomas wiped his mouth and faced the guard. "I was already out there. Why me?"

"Go into the ring." He handed him a mouth guard and stepped to the side to close the cage again.

Thomas's legs were heavy as he clambered through the ropes. Slowly, he bandaged his hands, hoping, praying that his opponent would be an amateur like Etienne. He closed his eyes and prayed to see Charlene again, if he managed to survive the next fight. The thought of losing her terrified him. A friend had once told him that only a man who has something to lose knows what to fight for.

Thomas wasn't afraid to die. As a soldier, as well as an ATF agent, he had risked his life many times. However, he didn't want to die here, now, at the hands of an unknown adversary, who wasn't an enemy but a man forced into the same inescapable situation.

The second fighter parted the ropes and entered the ring. He was six feet tall and built like a swimmer, with broad shoulders and small hips. His long arms featured massive bicep muscles, which he flexed while he warmed up. Thomas read in his eyes that this fight was business—he would deliver a quick series of blows leading to the inevitable knockout so that he could leave again as a winner. Unlike other men, who studied their opponents, he looked around the arena, pretending equanimity.

The referee shouted, "And here we have Jules, winner of the last tournament! Welcome back, Jules!"

This time, Thomas didn't turn to see the glee in Tyrone's eyes.

The bell rang. Jules made a threatening step forward, fists raised and ready to smash everything that was in his way.

"Any news about Raiden Stroud?" Nicolas asked. "Did his pictures show on the Darknet?"

"No. We received pictures of him from a friend for comparison, and Lesley added some details about his physique — the ones that don't show on normal pictures — but neither the program nor Agent Arpin have found him yet."

"Why not? He's such an outstanding specimen, customers would stand in line for him."

"Either the time was too short — he was kidnapped five days ago — or he's already been sold without any display on the net. Remember, the Chinese man appeared to have an interest in him, as Lesley pointed out. Maybe this kidnapping was . . . how shall I put it?"

"A kidnapping *on demand*?" Nicolas asked, disgusted.

"Yes, something like that." Christina made a sound of disappointment. "We keep looking, Nicolas."

Nicolas wiped his face. Behind him, Jason shouted his name. "I've got to go. Please, call me anytime you want, but bring me good news."

"Will do."

Jules danced around the ring, nimble as any professional

boxer with a five-day training routine. He moved around Thomas, delivered a few jabs and punches into his enemy's defense, but they were simply meant to tease Thomas, maybe to annoy him. Thomas didn't take the bait. He reserved his dwindling strength for the one moment that might grant him a chance for a precise punch.

Thomas evaded time and again, but also had to take some hard blows when he didn't anticipate his opponent's moves. He hoped he would make it into round two and that Jules might lose his temper. Jules's focus was fixed on Thomas's face. As if sensing Thomas's plan, he lashed out to hit Thomas's midsection with a well-timed jab. Immediately, Thomas saw double, and the pain was stronger than being shot in the gut. His knees buckled, and his fists dropped.

He knew that Jules would go for his face right before the first punch hit his cheekbone. His nose broke with the next blow, and he couldn't breathe. Blood gushed across his lips and chin. He went down and tried to cover his face with his hands. Jules pounded his fists against his kidneys and spleen, and every strike was like a knife cutting through his body. The agony spread through Thomas like a fast rolling wave that enclosed him, took him away, made him wish he could vanish. He couldn't see anymore. The sounds around came from afar. Still, Jules's fists hammered on his body, even though Thomas wasn't close to getting back on his feet. He tried to curl up but found no protection.

After uncounted seconds and harder blows, the referee sounded the bell. Thomas sucked in air through his split lips and spat out the mouth guard. His consciousness reeled when the referee announced Jules as the winner of the fight. While the crowd cheered and whistled enthusiastically, Thomas passed out.

A group of rich-looking people in classy clothing entered the hall to check the young men up and down while they slurped champagne from crystal glasses. Raiden saw the hunger in their eyes as their gazes switched from the victims' faces to their crotches. One man wiped his mouth, another licked his lips as if he had seen some exquisite food he wanted to taste. Several guests approached the victims to have a closer look and touch, smiling at the men's vain attempts to dodge the intimacies. One man touched the prisoner's long black hair as if testing its softness and laughed out loud when the captive writhed in the tethers.

When he turned his head as far as he could, Raiden saw a monitor mounted close to his position. The film showed him under the shower as he tried to get an erection. The scene repeated in loops, only interrupted by close-up pictures and a few text lines about Raiden's age and parentage. Horrified, he turned back, but now he understood the Player's clever planning. The audience was agitated after the fights in the arena — the cheering had been loud enough to penetrate the closed doors — and eager to get into more personal contact. To satisfy their needs, the boss displayed young victims so that the customers could watch them twist in their tethers. Judging by the guests' appearance, money was something they had in abundance and wouldn't talk about. Though Raiden didn't recognize any of them, it was a fair bet that there were several dignitaries among them.

Now that the effect of the narcotic had worn off, Raiden retched. His stomach churned even though he hadn't eaten all day. He hung his head, but the collar pressed on his Adam's apple, and the feeling worsened. He looked back up, straight into the eyes of a middle-aged Chinese man in a black suit, white dress shirt, and dark red tie, who scrutinized him through thick glasses. Breathing heavily, the man used a white handkerchief to blot sweat off his brow. Mumbling words Raiden didn't understand but interpreted as curses, the Chinese man adjusted his glasses and ran his sweaty fingers down Raiden's clothes. He seemed pleased that the prisoner shuddered with disgust. Then the man activated his cell phone, but the second he pressed the dial button, a guard moved in and told him that phones were forbidden. The guard was unimpressed by the customer's outburst and asked him politely and yet unmistakably to leave the room.

Raiden counted fourteen men and one woman who strolled through the showroom as if they were selecting a new boat at a fair. They were chatting and laughing, welcoming those they knew and making polite conversation with others. The moment he met the gaze of a fat man in his forties with beady eyes and an unhealthy red face, Raiden realized these people wouldn't be showing their faces if it was possible that the victims could identify them to the FBI. The insight destroyed his hopes that he would ever be released. He wouldn't leave the room as a free man, but as the prisoner of yet another kidnapper like the Player. Now he understood Thomas's and Miguel's worried glances. They had known about Raiden's fate and decided not to tell him. He was devastated to learn that at this place he wasn't a human being but an object someone with money would purchase. Never before had he wished to have left with his parents for Spain. Now he longed to see his mom and dad again, to feel their protective hands on him. *How the hell did I get into this situation?*

The Chinese man returned, still agitated, still with a temper he barely controlled. He was sweating profusely and pushing back the glasses that kept slipping off his nose. After another critical look at Raiden's physique, he stepped around him to look at his back, then asked a question. The guard shook his head. Raiden couldn't tell whether the guard didn't understand the language or had no answer. Frustrated and mumbling to himself, the man left to contact another man with a nametag to bother him with questions.

Raiden's imagination ran wild — would he be transported to the Chinese man's home? Would he serve as a fighter in another illegal fight club? Would he spend his time in a brothel for Asians, who preferred an exotic man like him? Once more, he was close to retching. He tried to unclench his fists, took deep breaths and forced himself to observe the crowd rather than speculate on his fate. Given the way he was shackled, he couldn't free himself.

Farther to the left, the Chinese man had a heated discussion with the tall man who worked for the Player. They watched several rows of pictures on a tablet, and the Chinese man appeared more at ease afterward but still disconcerted. He pointed at Raiden and held up his phone. The assistant shook his head. As if called by an urgent voice, the Player entered the room, greeted his guests, and bowed his head toward the angry Chinese man. He took over the conversation, smiling, nodding. The man didn't appear satisfied with the result, threw a last glance at Raiden, and left the room.

The Player took a glass of champagne and came over, obviously in a splendid mood.

"You're causing quite a stir," he said cheerfully while his hand stroked Raiden's ribcage in a loving way. "If I had more specimens like you, I'd be a millionaire." He laughed and encased Raiden's crotch with his soft, warm hand. "But then, if you were no longer special, prices might drop." The Player squeezed and kept the pressure until Raiden bit the gag, groaning. "Isn't that what you want? Pain and more pain?" He drank champagne and kept eye contact while he clenched and unclenched his hand. "That's what you thrive on, right? I wrote in your profile that you need a rigorous hand and that you like the agony of tight tethers. I wonder why you don't have a hard-on. I admit I expected you to live up to the occasion."

The Player let go, set down the glass, and used the wet cloth his assistant handed him to wipe his hands. "You don't want to be a disappointment, right? I considered you the highlight of tonight's show." Without further ado, the Player turned to the next man in line and touched him the same way. The prisoner whined with fear as much as revulsion.

Raiden was still digesting the pain when the only female interested party approached him, head cocked and smiling invitingly. She wore a shimmering black evening dress that emphasized her female curves. Her dark brown hair was combed back and held in a bun. Small earrings and a matching necklace testified to good taste and money. She wasn't a beauty in the true sense of the meaning, but an attractive woman in her forties with lively brown eyes. After a brief glance at the Player's back, she moved closer in her high heels, and Raiden tried to speak around the gag, but the tongue depressor prohibited any communication. He was frustrated. She stepped around him, opened the *Velcro*, and let the gag slip out of his mouth to present it to him on her index finger.

"Better this way?"

"Yes. Thank you. Listen, you have to—"

"What's your game?" she asked, twirling the gag around her finger and making a face as if she was speaking about sports. When the guard approached, she held up a hand, stopping him.

"You have to help—"

"You love pain, as I read." She pointed toward the monitor. "You're wearing nipple rings, right?" She opened the top buttons of his dress shirt to reach inside. "Oh, that's lovely." She pulled one ring, not gently.

Raiden grimaced. "Not like this. Please . . ." He clenched his fists, cursing that he couldn't make a step in her direction.

"What's your preferred position?" She cocked her head. "Are you a stallion—take your girl from behind?"

"No, I don't—" He tore at the shackles, but his fury appeared to amuse her.

"Conservative? Missionary style?" She sounded disappointed. "Or even leave the leading role to the girl?"

"Listen, please, I don't—"

"Ssh." She put a hand on his cheek and gently stroked his hair. "Wow, so soft. You're quite a catch. I'm thinking about buying you and wonder whether you're worth the money."

"Worth your money?" His voice boomed through the room loud enough that the guests turned their heads and stopped talking. The woman stepped away from him. "You fucking bitch! I was torn away from my life! I was thrown in a cell and maltreated, and you think about your fucking money?"

Wide-eyed, the woman handed the next guard the gag, but she didn't turn away fast enough to escape the Player's attention.

"Isn't there anyone in this room with a conscience?" Raiden rattled the shackles again, knowing he couldn't break them but unable to hold still. The chains went taut, and the metal column hummed with the strain. "Are there only fucking criminals in this room?"

The Player made a gesture, but the guard had already pressed the gag between Raiden's teeth.

Frustrated beyond measure, Raiden snorted and wished he could have spat at the woman's confused face.

The Player grabbed the woman's upper arm and hissed, "Yolana, what do you think you're doing?"

"I just wanted to hear his voice!" she shouted and broke his grip. "Don't tell me this is a divine service by now. I know you better."

"If you want a meeting with one of the objects on display, you can talk with me, and we make an arrangement. In private! This isn't the right place for your solo!"

"Fine. Tell me where and when, and I'll be there." She

raised her brows, challenging him.

"It's a day too late for that. You knew that in advance. He's on the list for tonight. You either bid or you leave it." He turned around, made sure Raiden's gag was fastened, and went back to the guests he had been talking with.

Yolana pursed her lips and ran her fingers along her décolleté. Now that the Player was occupied elsewhere, she regained her equanimity. "You don't know who I am, right?" She came closer once more and reached around his body to touch his buttocks through the fabric. "I'm the DA's widow, and I've been longing to see someone like you for a long time."

Raiden panted and wished he could bite her nose. Her hand reached further down along his thigh and back up toward his crotch. Under different circumstances, her touching would arouse him. He was nauseated at the amount of disrespect for human dignity.

Yolana simpered, and the fine lines around her eyes deepened. "You're very well trained, and you've got a temper I like." She ran her painted nails along the line of buttons. "I have a special place for you." She glanced over her shoulder. "I promise, you'll be happy with me." She sighed, as if imagining her time with him. "Maybe I'll place a bid." After a moment, she nodded to herself. "Oh, yes, I think I'll definitely place a bid."

Raiden's belief in the good of humankind was collapsing, and he couldn't do anything to alter his fate.

Thomas opened the eye that wasn't swollen shut to look at a gray ceiling where lights were flashing now and then. He heard an engine running. A moment later, he realized he was being transported in a large van that was causing the rocking motion. Two men in the driver's cabin spoke with each other. Thomas didn't understand every word but learned from the context that he had been brought to a kind of institution where people were already waiting for him. Slowly, because every movement hurt, he lifted his head a fraction. He was strapped to a stretcher, had a breathing mask on his face, and a needle in his left arm. Obviously, he was being fed with glucose. The bandages around his hands were gone.

It seemed like an unexpected act of mercy that he wasn't buried in a lonely place, but then the Player wouldn't risk taking him to a public hospital. Thomas shivered. He had come so far and was still alive. He would do what was in his power to survive this ordeal. But then, the pain in his kidneys was agonizing. He tried to stay conscious so he could hear the men's conversation. For a fleeting moment, he succeeded, but the van hit a pothole and the pain skyrocketed.

He passed out again.

Raiden had always wanted to feel alive, to taste life to its full extent. Raised without the troubles of many teenagers, Raiden had time to study, to live his fantasies, and to have fun with girls. While his friends talked about lacking money, about their close-fisted parents, about their bad looks and even more about their bad luck with women, Raiden had it all and enjoyed it all.

During a love night with a trained mixed-martial-arts fighter he had met after a tournament, Raiden sensed that she was stronger than she admitted. He had challenged her to a play-fight on the bed and teased her not to hold back. She tussled with a better technique than he expected and had the upper hand within minutes. She pushed him on his belly and held his arm in a painfully tight grip while she pressed one knee against his shoulder blade. Raiden felt the discomfort increase the more she drew back his arm, and the pain was sweet and arousing. He had an erection and didn't ask her to stop until she let go with a frustrated sigh.

He asked her to do it again and explained what he'd experienced, but she considered him a freak and left in a hurry.

He was seventeen-years-old.

The Player announced that the auction would start in fifteen minutes so the guests used the time to have another, even closer look at the six prisoners on display.

Raiden hung his head, exhausted, trembling with strain. He closed his eyes when yet another interested party let his fingers pass over his bicep muscles, humming with interest.

"He's really a specialty," the stranger said to the man standing next to him. He sounded out of breath. "In every way. I wonder where our host finds those men."

"He has his ways," the other man said and laughed a deep laugh, full of content. "Many secret ways."

"Let's hope he can keep them open. I can't wait for the bidding to start."

Thomas woke up when the van stopped. The men in the front were quarreling with each other.

"We have to get away! I don't want to be stopped with him in the back!" The man's voice was high with agitation. "That wasn't the plan, and no one pays me when we end up in jail!"

"If we turn the car now, they'll definitely stop us," the second man said calmly. "No. We wait and hope to get by undetected."

"It won't work, man. It won't work. Fuck!" The man slammed the dashboard. "You chose the route!"

"Don't say this is my fault! I didn't call the police to have the street blocked. Who knows what they're doing here? It's a traffic checkpoint, nothing else."

"And why are they armed to their teeth? No, Charlie,

they're on a manhunt."

Thomas lay very still, knowing that any movement would send him straight back into that unhealthy slumber he had come from.

The van rolled slowly, then stopped again. Thomas strained to hear the police officer talk to the driver. Politely and yet firmly, he asked for the papers and the license. After a minute, the officer ordered the driver to get out and open the back doors.

"What're you searching for?" the driver asked. "Did you lose someone?"

It was meant as a joke, but the officer's voice was hard and unrelenting. "Open the back doors."

"Okay, okay." The driver got out and walked along the car.

Thomas held his breath when the pain got so intense, he feared he'd pass out any moment. His lower body seemed to be a sea of fire, so hot that it was consuming the rest of his body wave by agonizing wave. He wished that the officer would hurry to him. He wanted to see Charlene again, and now he had hope that this miracle would happen.

The doors opened, and the officer clambered into the cargo area. "Oh, my God! What happened to you, sir?"

The driver cursed viciously.

Thomas didn't make a move even though he wanted to urge the officer to help him.

"Call an ambulance! Right now! Hurry!" the officer shouted to his colleagues who waited outside. "And arrest those bastards!"

Thomas breathed as lightly as he could, and when the officer knelt beside him, tried to signal him to take away the mask.

"It's all right, sir," the officer said soothingly as he pulled the mask off Thomas's nose. "You'll make it. A doc will be here shortly."

"Tell the FBI," Thomas whispered. "Tyrone Turner."

"All right, yes, will do. Please, don't move. Can you tell me your name and what happened to you?"

Thomas parted his lips. A heartbeat later, he gathered his strength to say, "Tell my wife that I love her. Will always."

"Sir? Sir!"

Thomas closed his eyes and let out his breath.

The Native American's long black hair was shining in the spotlight, which was on his body while the rest of the room lay in semi-darkness. Close to him, the Player stood with a microphone to announce the man's sizes and abilities and then opened the auction, praising the subject with eloquent phrases. He sounded sincere and dignified, like any legal executive advertising his merchandise. One of his helpers stood at a desk with a gavel in his right hand and confirmed the guests' bids. The numbers were by far higher than at any exclusive car dealer, the high-priced models included. The high-speed bidding went on for two minutes, and the fat man with the red face won the bid. His joyful exclamation *Yes!* caused laughter in the audience.

"And there goes another lucky client." Smiling broadly, the Player pointed at the fat man and raised his thumb, then made three steps toward Raiden, and the spotlight followed. "The words *exotic* and *unique* were used to describe this last specimen. He's twenty-five years old, of Hawaiian and Spanish parentage, and as you can see, he's in his prime. He'll be the jewel in every collection." The Player bared his teeth at the expectant crowd. "Well, enough said. Please, place your bids for this outstanding servant."

When he had turned off the microphone, he bent to Raiden to whisper, "Let's see whether my Chinese client truly wants you."

CHAPTER ELEVEN

In the silence that followed, Raiden still heard the voices of the excited crowd and the numbers the auctioneer shouted with growing enthusiasm. When the last bid had been placed by the Chinese man to trump the only female bidder, the Player nodded his appreciation when the gavel's fall finished the auction.

Once more, the Chinese man approached Raiden at the column, now smiling contentedly. While a guard cleaned Raiden's face, the Player joined the client and listened to his demands for delivery.

The man made a decisive gesture with his flat hand, saying, "No changes this time. You will deliver the object without any changes, and you will deliver it on time. If this doesn't happen, you will face the consequences."

The Player simpered. "We all will face the consequences of our doings, won't we?"

The guard freed Raiden from the last shackles and pushed him into his cell, then locked the door. When his steps abated, Raiden slipped to the floor and covered his face with his hands so that Miguel wouldn't see him cry. *Sold like a boat, a car, a piece of jewelry.* He couldn't grasp the ferocity of the customers — one of them the widow of the DA! How could a group of people act without morals, without humanity? How was it possible that those dignitaries walked around, carefree and confident that the police wouldn't arrest them? Had he left the twenty-first century for the Middle Ages, where slavery was a common business again?

Raiden thought over what had just happened. He had felt as if the gavel hit him directly in the head, pushed him through an unseen wall and out of the world he knew. Still shackled to the column, he had retched and spat bile while the crowd got up from their chairs to either leave the room or congratulate the Chinese bidder for his outstanding purchase. Waiters in white shirts and black vests had served more champagne, their faces as blank as those of the Players' assistants. The Player had mingled with the guests again — laughing merrily about their jokes — and answered questions concerning transportation and time schedules. Judging by the confidence with which he'd spoken, he had done this many times before and knew exactly how to cloak a prisoner transport and escape police prosecution.

When Raiden regained his composure, he went to fetch a cup of water. Miguel sat on the cot, holding his plate with food without eating.

"Where's Tom?" Raiden asked.

Miguel glanced at him and shook his head.

"He's not coming back?"

Once again, he shook his head.

Raiden looked into the empty cell. Thomas had left nothing behind, no personal items a relative would claim. He was gone, and someone had cleaned the cell so that it was ready for another inmate.

"How . . ."

Miguel's tone betrayed his blunt words. "He smashed the nose of the first man he fought — the arrogant guy behind me. One blow to the nose, the next to his temple. *Boom*. He dropped like a stone. But that wasn't enough. He had to fight another one — Jules the *Monster*, who took him apart, piece by piece. Tom went down and was still knocked out when he was dragged out of the ring."

"Did they take him to a hospital?"

Miguel waved his hand, but the sadness in his eyes told that Raiden shouldn't count on it. "And you?"

Again, tears trickled down Raiden's cheeks. He had hoped Tom would be there to give him advice, to cheer him up or at least to share his misery. Raiden had never felt so alone in his life. Moreover, he feared that if Tom, who was a trained fighter, lost battles in this prison, he wouldn't stand a chance of surviving his fate.

"I was sold to a fucking Chinese man, and if I have it right, he paid a lot more money for me than he wanted."

"Sold, huh, pretty boy? At least you don't have to fight."

Raiden was at the bars in no time and clenched the metal as if to rip the bars apart. He bared his teeth. "Did you hear what I said? I was sold like some fucking boat! Someone will come and take me to God-knows-where! Do you think that's a better fate than being knocked out in the ring?"

Miguel smacked his lips, as if the alternative was tempting.

"It's not!" Raiden pressed his face between two bars and shouted even louder. "I'll be someone's toy! Think about that and tell me whether you want to take my place, you idiot!"

Miguel's eyes narrowed, and his lips were a thin line. His voice sank to a growl. "I wasn't looking for this here, either. I thought I'd fight like I did in my village. But this—this is a prison. Tom understood that faster than I did. You—you have a totally different fate. Who knows what awaits you?"

Raiden shook his head, his rage blown away as fast as it had come. While his heart beat painfully in his throat, his despair grew. "You didn't see them. The hunger. The greed." He wiped his face and pushed back his hair. "We were auctioned, one man after the other, and now I'm no longer master of my fate." He hung his arms through the bars and faced the floor of the adjacent cell. "During the auction, I couldn't believe what I heard. I didn't understand that the crowd consisted of down-and-dirty criminals. They'd come to take one of us . . . home, or wherever these people will keep their victims." Suddenly, strength left him and he sat on the cold floor again. The walls around him seemed to narrow inch by inch. It wouldn't take long before they would press on his body until he couldn't breathe anymore. "I don't know how to end this — to get away. I can't imagine that a man holds power over me and that I can do nothing to stop him."

"You don't know that."

Raiden hid his face behind his hands. "I know I've never been this deep in shit before."

Nicolas picked up the phone at the first ring when he identified the caller's number. "What have you for me?"

"A good morning to you, Nicolas." Christina's voice was void of emotion. "I've nothing concerning Raiden Stroud, but it could be that the police in Tuscaloosa, Alabama, found Thomas Zutarski. Maybe. I'm not sure yet."

"How is he?"

When the pause stretched, Nicolas repeated the question.

"The man was found in a van, badly wounded. He died before the ambulance arrived. I tried to reach Agent Freeman for the identification, but he's absent."

Nicolas closed his eyes and paused until he trusted his voice. "Yes, I know. He's out of town, working on a case for the ATF."

"And I learned from Mrs. Freeman that his wife, Charlene, wouldn't be able to come to the morgue."

"Thomas's body was already transported to DC?"

"On my request, yes. Again, we are not completely sure it's Thomas. Not until a related party has identified him."

Nicolas took a deep breath. When he looked in his partner's direction, Jason met his gaze. "I'll do it."

"Thank you."

"How come he was found in Tuscaloosa?"

"The local police were looking for a fugitive and had erected a roadblock. When the officers checked the van, they found a man tied to a stretcher. The officer called an ambulance, but it was too late. Since they're connected with the local FBI, they reported the incident. The agents called me because of my global alert concerning the kidnapping victims. After the formalities were done, I arranged for the victim and the drivers to be transferred to DC."

"Thank you, Christina. That's —"

"Don't mention it. I hope it's not Thomas. Meet me after you've been to the morgue."

Nicolas put down the receiver. "Jason? Would you accompany me, please?"

Raiden stared at the food his captors provided. He was hungry but also disinterested in feeding his body. Every time he heard movement on the corridor, he feared he'd be fetched and transported to the man who'd bought him. The stress caused his stomach to turn over and over, but when the hunger became unbearable, he ate a few mouthfuls, listening to the sounds around. He was on edge when the guards delivered a new poor soul to the cell next to his. The young man collapsed on the cot and didn't react to the guards' bellowed orders. Then the helpers looked at Raiden in a way that made him hold his breath. As if knowing his thoughts, the guards curled their lips into vicious smiles and went away.

Raiden let go of the breath he had been holding. Whatever his desolate situation now, he knew it would be worse wherever he was taken.

The coroner was a friendly man in his fifties, round-faced and portly. He wore silver-rimmed glasses and looked recently shaven. His freshly-pressed lab coat rustled when he rounded the corner of his crowded desk. After the introduction, he led Nicolas and Jason into the cool examination room.

"Are you sure you want to see the body? I asked for his superior for a reason." Dr. Bryson frowned and hesitated with the hand at the corner of the white cloth covering the body. "You said you were his friend—"

"His superior's out of town and I volunteered. His wife wouldn't be able to stand the sight."

"I see. Believe me, I know you've seen a lot, but this is—"

"Get it over with, please."

Jason watched with interest as the doctor pulled back the white linen. Thomas's face was so bloody that not all the injuries were clearly visible. Jason could tell that many of the wounds resulted from severe beatings. His wrists bore the distinctive signs of long-worn shackles. While he stared at the many injuries that spoke a language of violence in capital letters, Nicolas made an indescribable sound in his throat Jason had never heard before. Quick-wittedly, he reached out and kept his friend from falling.

"Sit down!" Jason wasn't the strongest man, and keeping his much taller friend from hitting the floor was an effort. He slowed Nicolas's fall and crouched beside him. "Nick? Hey, talk to me."

Nicolas's face was pale and sweaty, his voice but a breath. "It's Thomas. They tortured him to death."

The medical examiner sighed. "That's partly correct, but the multiple injuries result from knuckle fights. The last one, I assume, was a severe one without rules. The cause of death was internal bleeding. A blow ruptured his spleen, and the man who did this had enormous strength. Given his condition, I assume the victim died within two or three hours after the fight."

Jason looked up pleadingly. "We understand. Please, send us the report ASAP with all details you find. They might lead us directly to the killers."

"Will do." He hesitated. "Does your friend need something? Smelling salts, maybe?"

Nicolas took a shaky breath. "I'll make it. I just need a moment."

Jason braced to bring Nicolas back on his feet. He glanced at the coroner. "Cover the body first." He supported Nicolas and helped him stand. "Lean on me, and let's get out of here."

He took Nicolas to the men's room. As he turned on the cold water, he saw tears on Nicolas's cheeks.

"I'm sorry, Nick, really sorry. I know he was a good friend."

"How shall I tell Charlene? She's six months pregnant." He splashed his face with water. "She needs him. She had a nervous breakdown when he was kidnapped, and her doc fears for the baby." Nicolas hid his face behind his hands, sobbing. "There are no words to explain what happened to him. She'll never recover."

The news of Charlene's pregnancy hit Jason hard. His wife, Elaine, had just learned she was pregnant with her first child and was very excited. He failed to imagine what Elaine would do if given the news of her husband killed off-duty. He also failed to imagine what ordeal Thomas had lived through and how much he had wished to return to his wife.

He put a hand on Nicolas's shoulder. "You're right. There's nothing you can say or do to soften the blow. You can be there for her, that's all."

Nicolas straightened and reached for a paper towel to dry his face. Though still pale, he was regaining his composure.

"If you don't mind, I'd like to drive to Vernon's place right away. I can't delay the news for another hour."

On the way out Jason asked, "Does she have someone she could call? A sister, a friend? She shouldn't be alone."

"She's staying with Thomas's superior and his wife. Thomas and Charlene took refuge with them after Charlene left Florence Town."

Without discussing it, Jason took over driving.

Raiden sat with his legs drawn up, shivering though it wasn't cold. From downstairs, he heard the helpers call the victims to leave their cells. Chains were jingling as the men were tied to each other and led away toward the next wing.

Steps were getting closer, and Raiden looked into the hard, emotionless faces of three guards.

"It's time. Your shuttle is here."

Raiden didn't move. For the life of him, he wouldn't make it easy for his captors to send him into even deeper misery.

The guards sensed the challenge, and two of them entered the cell, cudgels in their hands. "You have no chance against us, asshole. Move!"

Raiden sat in the corner, delaying his fate, even if it was only for a few minutes. His fear erupted in an attempt at pushing himself through his adversaries. He threw himself forward, determined to overthrow his captors so that they stood in each other's way. He rammed his head against the first man's midsection, made him step back, and that way blocked his partner's raised arm with the cudgel. Raiden ignored the pain of a punch against his kidneys. He didn't think. He hit the man's genitals, heard his scream, and pushed forward so that the second guard flew against the bars. Never before in his life had Raiden fought with such passion. He reached the open door, where the third guard waited. Behind him, the two men cursed and got back to their feet, one of them complaining in a high, pain-filled voice. As he faced the third enemy, Raiden conceived that the short stick in his left hand wasn't a cudgel but a cattle prod. Driven by the single thought to escape his fate, Raiden dodged the first attack but landed hard on his right knee. The guard charged him again, this time even quicker.

Behind him, the second guard was back in the fight, still cursing under his breath.

Raiden reached for the guard's hand to get control over the cattle prod, but the man anticipated the move, evaded to the left, and hit Raiden hard below his ribcage. From one second to the next, Raiden's right side was on fire as the high voltage shocked his body. He screamed, breathless, and went down, weak and beaten. When he tried to get up, a second hit robbed him of his strength and sent him down on the floor where he lay panting.

"Did you think you'd get away with that?" The first guard was about to kick him when the second man interfered. "Don't tell me—"

"Unharmed," the guard said as he put a belt around Raiden's waist. "The boss was precise about that. Any scratch, and he'll make you pay." He turned Raiden on his back to fasten handcuffs and ankle cuffs. "He said that he made three times the money he had anticipated. Every bruise or scratch would lessen the man's value." He looked at Raiden again. "You're the *Specimen of the Week*, so to speak. Up with you."

"Where are you taking me?" Raiden's speech slurred. "Tell me."

The guards helped Raiden stand on his feet.

"You're going to meet your new family."

"Who—"

"Shut up!"

The guards led him downstairs to a gray van with the back

doors wide open. Raiden stepped back seeing the bench with the collar on a chain.

"No! Don't put me in there!"

"You don't have a choice! Go!"

In spite of his limited leeway, Raiden fought the men with all he had until they wrestled him toward the van. A fourth man supported them, using a cattle prod. Together they pushed Raiden into the cargo area. In a hurry, they locked the collar around his neck and secured his ankles. Done, the guards let out their collective breaths.

Sobbing and giving into his defeat, Raiden hung his head. The doors were locked then the engine came to life. The van rumbled across a stony path until it reached a street and accelerated.

During the ride, Raiden's memory took him back to the morning with Lesley.

He had accepted the invitation to join her for breakfast at her friends' home as a surprising development in their relationship, a decision he didn't question so as not to ruin her exuberant mood. Giddy like a teenager, she had chosen the pet's outfit and added the bone-gag, laughing merrily. Raiden was content to come along, in spite of the outfit or that he might attract the neighbors. To be with Lesley, to see her laugh and enjoy the time with him was worth every costume and feeling cold throughout the ride. He had crawled into the van, and Lesley slapped his bare butt in an affectionate way, telling him how much she looked forward to seeing Jacky's and Nick's faces. It had been a joyful morning — a bondage session with extras and the chance to meet with a likeminded couple.

Raiden tried to change his position, but the collar was tight and the chain too short. While the van sped toward its destination, Raiden was bereft of any possibility to take his fate into his own hands.

Jason tried to talk Nicolas out of visiting Agent Lawry right after he had delivered the news of Thomas's death to Charlene and an equally sad Teresa Freeman. Jason couldn't remember any time that his partner had looked so pale and hollow, beaten to the ground by an enemy he didn't know and couldn't fight.

"I'm sure she'll send you her findings," Jason said as he parked the car at the parking lot. "You should take a break, buddy. You look like shit."

"I promised Charlene I'll solve Tom's murder."

Nicolas left the car, and Jason hurried along at his side. Since they had left the morgue, Nicolas's blood pressure seemed to be dangerously low. Not for the first time since they had become partners, Jason feared Nicolas would collapse.

"I hear your words but don't believe them. First, you've got your own case to work on. Second, you can't make promises you can't keep. Who knows where the gangsters are?"

"Then I'll find them." Nicolas entered Christina's office, and Jason trailed along like an unwanted attachment.

"I already know that you identified Thomas," Christina said instead of a greeting. "I'm sorry for your loss."

Nicolas nodded, and when Jason urged him, he sat on the chair close to Christina's desk.

Only for Christina to see, Jason mouthed, *He's in a bad shape.*

"Let me set this straight, Nicolas," Christina began. "Even though Thomas was killed and we have a lead to his killers,

Sullivan's order still stands. I can share my results of the investigation with you, but that's it." She waited for Nicolas to agree, but he stared at her without saying a word. "Moving on. I have the driver's and his companion's statement concerning the transport of Agent Zutarski." She opened the file. "After telling them that they were responsible for manslaughter, Ray Simmons—he drove the van—and Charlie Kent decided to cooperate. They claimed they received the victim at a parking lot close to Anniston in Alabama with orders to take him to Moundville, south of Tuscaloosa. They didn't know the men who delivered the victim or where they came from. The description wasn't precise, either, but both said that the exchange was made at night and the two men wore hoods. I sent agents to search the area and the parking lot, so far without results. It's obvious Simmons and Kent had no idea where the victim came from or who had beaten him. The facility in Moundville is a private clinic." She looked up from the file and hesitated before finally saying quietly, "They specialize in organ transplantation."

Nicolas put a hand over his eyes. "That's why they kept him alive. Oh, my god."

"Right." Christina inclined her head, a sympathetic frown on her face. "The clinic is next in line to have visitors from the FBI. I bet there's more behind it, but that's another case. Simmons described a dark gray van with Georgia license plates without knowing the exact numbers, so the FBI bureau in Atlanta is on it."

Nicolas wiped his chin. "But they don't know where to start, right? We still have no clue where Thomas was kept. Did the coroner send you his report?"

"It's not here yet. But there's something else you should know. The officer who entered the van wrote down that Thomas said to him, quote, *Tell the FBI, Tyrone Turner.* And he asked the officer to tell his wife that he loved her." Once more, she waited for Nicolas to react. Breathing deeply, she went on. "I checked the information and found the case you worked on for the ATF. Tyrone Turner is still on the loose."

"And he's the one who put Tom into misery." Nicolas looked up pleadingly. "Tell me that you've got something about Tyrone's whereabouts. Any hint where he was or whom he joined?"

"Not at this time. We assume he's in league with the Gallego brothers, so we are concentrating our investigation in Georgia and intensifying the search for Tyrone Turner. His description was handed to every police station." She lifted a hand to stop Nicolas's question. "Yes, I'll give you a call if anything interesting pops up." She closed the file. "Go home, Nicolas. It's hard to cope with such a loss, and I bet your visit to the widow wasn't easy."

"Easy, huh?" Nicolas shook his head and slumped even deeper into the chair. "That was the hardest thing I ever had to do. She's fragile, Christina, she's like a small bird with thin bones that'll crack under the slightest pressure. She knew it was bad news when I entered the house, and she fell to her knees immediately. She couldn't stop crying, so Teresa called a doc." He wiped tears from his eyes. "Even when the doc gave her a mild sedative, she was still shaking her head and calling his name as if she could undo his death that way. I fear . . ." He broke off and turned his head away.

Jason wished he could lift the immense pressure off his partner's shoulders. He had stood beside him when he explained the circumstances of Thomas's death in a clipped version to Charlene, but the fact that she'd never see her husband again broke her heart. Nicolas had been taciturn during the ride. Jason knew it wasn't only his partner's mourning that weighed him down. Without knowing Charlene intimately, Jason assumed the young woman would be capable of taking her own life if she found it meaningless without Thomas at her side.

"Come on, buddy, I'll take you home." He looked at Christina. "Thank you for your help."

"I'll keep you in the loop. I know we're closing in. It's but a question of time."

CHAPTER TWELVE

Nicolas unlocked the door to his house and turned to Jason. "Thanks for taking me home and for your company. This was hard."

"I know." Jason put a hand on his shoulder.

Nicolas knew he should thank his partner for acting like a mother hen and not leaving his side throughout the afternoon, but he was too beaten down to find words.

"It's all right," Jason said, as if he had listened to Nicolas's inner monologue. "Say hello to Jacky for me."

Nicolas went inside, dropped the keys, and took off his shoes. He wanted to vanish in a hole and get away from the sadness and helplessness he had experienced, but there were Jacklyn and Lesley, and both deserved more than his silence.

"What happened?" Jacklyn asked.

The fear in her eyes touched Nicolas to the core. He took her in his arms and pressed her warm body against his, breathing the scent of her hair and her subtle perfume. He was overwhelmed with happiness that she was alive and could give back the embrace, while at the same time his sadness that Charlene would never again hold Thomas in her arms stole away his words. If Charlene found the strength to keep on living, the child would grow up without his father. No narrative about his friendship with Thomas would bring him back.

Lesley frowned as she approached them, and Nicolas embraced her, too. They stood for an immeasurable time until he got a grip on his emotion and recapped the circumstances of his friend's death. He left out many details, but the fact of his murder brought tears to both women's eyes.

Lesley sat on the couch and bit her lower lip. "Do you think they will kill Raiden, too?" she asked in a tearful voice. "Will he be . . ." She broke off, opening her hand, palm up.

"No." Nicolas sat down opposite her and tried to sound positive. "Agent Lawry assumes that men like Raiden aren't meant to be fighters but . . ." He rubbed his chin, unwilling to bring home more bad news. He had never before felt so wretched.

"You're saying he was kidnapped for his looks." Lesley seemed to find consolation that her lover's death wasn't imminent. "So, there will be people who want such a man for themselves. To keep him for pleasure."

"That's right." He couldn't look her in the eyes. His imagination created horrible pictures. He wanted to run and find Raiden and battle the enemies that kept him. If ever possible, he would fight with his fists, if only to vent this immeasurable amount of hatred accumulated in his body.

"That opens the possibility that he'll . . . change owners and be taken someplace else. Isn't there a way to find his whereabouts?"

"The FBI is looking for him and the other victims. Agent Lawry hopes that they'll find more details because of Tom's murder."

"I see." Lesley was trembling like a leaf.

Nicolas searched for words to console her, but he couldn't think of any.

The van stopped. Raiden looked up when he heard footsteps approaching. There was a snowball's chance in hell that his misery would end if he didn't take his fate into his own hands.

"Let me out! Please, let me out!" He had pleaded so often, his words sounded hollow, and his voice was hoarse.

A strong looking Chinese man opened the back doors and unlocked the collar and the chain at his ankle cuffs. He and a second man gestured for him to get out.

Raiden huffed and lifted his shackled hands. "Do you think I could fight like this?" He sucked in air through his clenched teeth as he sat on the van's rim and slipped to the ground carefully. His pretended he was in great pain when he straightened.

He stood in the back yard of a large manor with at least thirty rooms. The building seemed to be about a hundred years old, meant to represent a wealthy, southern family. One of the windows on the second floor was open, and the curtain billowed in the wind. In the shadow of a ceiling lamp, Raiden saw the outlines of a person.

"Go!" The guard poked Raiden's back with a cudgel.

"Where am I? What is this here?"

Trying to memorize as much as possible of his surroundings, Raiden made his way across a well-tended path through part of a large garden to the back entrance. One floor up, the corridors he walked matched the exclusive exterior. Carpets, tapestry, paintings — the house had been decorated by a person with taste and money, meant to impress visitors. Raiden looked left and right into the open rooms, but they were empty, the expensive furniture unused. The further he came, the more he had the impression that the Chinese man he had seen at the auction was the only occupant, accompanied by several taciturn henchmen, who would do anything for him if he snapped his fingers. He couldn't shake the image that this estate resided on a different planet, and that no one would ever know where he was, much less find him. It was devastating to know that he was lost to his family and friends. He was alone.

His muscles ached as he shuffled toward the end of the corridor. The large window allowed a stunning view into a huge illuminated garden with trimmed hedges, flower beds, and lounges protected by large parasols. In the darkness, he couldn't see where the garden ended and the road began.

In front of the last door, the men's strong hands pressed on his shoulders. He went down on his knees, grimacing when the pain in his legs returned. His stomach hurt, too. He couldn't remember when he had last eaten.

"Why —"

The Chinese man knocked the butt of the cudgel across the back of his head. "Quiet! Move."

Clenching his teeth, Raiden gave in and crawled across the soft woolen carpet. An old large walnut desk dominated the part of the room to his right, decorated with an illuminated globe and golden stationary. A brown leather armchair worth a president's office stood behind it. Walnut bookshelves stood along the walls. In between there were spaces for landscape paintings, tastefully illuminated by small lamps. A large window with a door to a balcony claimed the entire width of the room in front of him. The room smelled of leather and old books, but faintly of an exotic after-shave.

Two steps into the room, Raiden looked behind the desk and stopped, staring. The steel bars of a large cage shone in the light of a floor lamp. Close to it, a spanking bench with an additional wooden pillory for the feet waited to be used. Raiden's mouth went dry, his aches forgotten. Heart beating in his throat, he turned his head, but the Chinese guards kept him in view without urging him to get closer. *Is that a part of my destiny? Again being imprisoned by a lunatic?*

Raiden's hands clenched into tight fists as he thought about escape. Though the guards didn't appear to be seasoned fighters, they had weapons, and Raiden was shackled. He could attack and maybe overwhelm one of them, but the second one would beat him to the floor without blinking.

Raiden turned around when a Chinese man in his mid-forties entered through a door hidden between the bookshelves to his left. He was of short statue — about five feet — but unlike other small people, his head, arms, and legs were proportional to his shortness. He wore his black hair slicked back, had a slim mustache, and thin lips. His eyes spoke of intelligence, but Raiden discovered the same hunger and desire to possess and control a human being as he'd seen in the other guests at the auction. The man adjusted the sleeves of his dress shirt as he examined Raiden critically. The suit was tailored and didn't rustle as the man walked around Raiden. The scent of the exotic after-shave intensified.

"Very well." He made a contented sound. "As ordered, so delivered." His English bore a heavy accent, and the words came out as though they were chiseled in stone. "I waited for you for a long time."

Raiden lifted his head. "If you ask me, you could've waited even longer."

"Ah, the insults of a newly arrived servant." He simpered and clapped his small hands. "How enchanting." The false smile vanished. "No, don't think about attacking me. My men will overwhelm you and tie you up if you show any aggressive behavior. I've seen it all before. So don't be tempted to make a move just because I am small." He continued walking around Raiden as if to take in every detail of his body. "Let me make this clear, one time only." He arrived in front of Raiden to look him in the eyes. "I'm your master. You will call me master. You will not insult me, contradict me, or spit at me. From this night on, you will serve me, and you will not by any means act against me."

Raiden shuddered with disgust. "You can't—"

The cudgel hit Raiden's thigh hard enough that it stung. He grunted and made eye contact with the guard, who was now swinging the cudgel in his hand, eyes narrow, brows twitching.

The master went on as if Raiden hadn't spoken. "Any kind

of disobedience will be punished. I will choose the measure and the way of your punishment. It can be isolation, restrictions, hunger and thirst—believe me, I trained many servants, and none of them dared to act against me more than once."

He simpered, obviously satisfied that Raiden held his tongue, and signaled his flunky standing at the door.

"The first days, you will spend in a small cell so that you get acquainted with the new surroundings."

"You mean a kennel? I'm not a dog you bought."

This time, the cudgel hit the sole of his foot. Raiden bit his lips trying to not cry out and grant his captor the satisfaction of having hurt him.

"I will help your unruly tongue."

Raiden expected a gag, but instead the guard locked a collar around his neck. It was made of a rough fabric with two oblong parts that pressed against the sides of his Adam's apple. Raiden swallowed and coughed when he felt the collar tighten.

"This was a gift from the man some call the *Player*. He gave it to me when our business situation was better than it is now." He cleared his throat and straightened the cuffs of his shirt again. After a pause he used to examine the bruise Raiden had suffered from the guard's attack, he said, "You'd better not try to speak now, or the voltage in this collar will hurt you much more than you anticipate."

Raiden looked up. He knew he should defy his captor's power over him but couldn't cloak his growing horror. Maybe a man like Thomas would have the stamina to laugh in the man's face, but Raiden lowered his chin, admitting his defeat. The master simpered and patted Raiden's head with the same affection people showed dogs.

"Hmm, you have very soft hair. A nice touch. Now that you understand your position, my men will prepare you for your stay." He straightened and addressed the guards in Chinese. His voice was angry when he added in English, "You can launch the attack now."

Some called him the *Joker*, some preferred the *King*, but if he had a choice, he'd love to be named *Two-Face,* the wild and tame opponent of Batman. Like him, the Player had moments of benevolence and those of raging madness if things didn't happen as planned. He could caress a woman's face and love her with devotion and kill a man in cold blood an hour later. He didn't want his partners to see his soft side. It would ruin his ruthless appeal. People must fear him, or he'd lose his influence and others would take over his business. Especially his Mexican partners were hungry and would kill their opponent over negligence. After the kidnapping of Thomas Zutarski, the Player had acted obligingly, but he had brought his point home when he threw out Tyrone and ordered his Mexican partners to make sure their obnoxious hyena would not return. Juan and Arturo understood the Player's threat to cut their business ties if they didn't do his bidding.

Standing at the window of his medieval apartment in the western wing of the premises, he mulled over the last conversation he had conducted with Mr. Wong and the barely hidden aggressiveness the man had displayed. Admittedly, the Player had exhausted his limits when he hadn't delivered Raiden to Mr. Cheng right away, but he was sure that the auction made up for that. As he knew, money wasn't a problem for Mr. Cheng, and the Player had hoped that this game spiced up their business arrangement. Then Mr. Cheng's assistant had been extraordinarily agitated after the auction, much more than was justified. The Player hadn't survived in his business for such a long time without the ability to anticipate his adversaries' moves.

He had ordered the guards to be extra careful now that Raiden had left the premises for Mr. Cheng's southern Georgia estate. The Player mused about what the Chinese man would do with his purchase — and what had happened to the specimen he had bought earlier the same year.

While he sat with a glass of bourbon, the guard at the northern entrance reported incoming vans. Immediately, the Player raised the alarm and had the premises lit up like a Christmas tree. If foreign enemies wanted to slip into his realm unseen, he would teach them better than to mess with him.

The guards were cautious around Raiden and didn't let him out of sight for a second when they opened the shackles and ordered him to take off his clothes. He was allowed to shower but not to get up. At first, Raiden assumed the guards expected an attack once they let him get on his feet, but soon realized he wasn't allowed to get up at all.

After the shower, a guard handed him long pants and a matching shirt in a soft yellow. When he looked up, a third guard appeared with two handfuls of chains and lockable shackles. Raiden groaned. The device was meant to restrict his movements so that he would be unable to put up a fight. Satisfied with the result, the guards led him downstairs again and into a large room with four separate cells, supervised by video surveillance from different angles. Raiden bet that the small Chinese man — *the Master* — had monitors to watch his prey's every move. The cells had bars on all sides, so the men had no private sphere, no corner to hide.

The cell to the right — equipped with a mattress and a bucket — was empty. Raiden was shooed inside and the door locked. When he turned around and signaled the guards that he wanted the shackles taken off, they grinned at him and turned away, talking in Chinese with each other, laughing. Both lit cigarettes and appeared at ease as they crossed the corridor.

Raiden slumped on the ground, exhausted and hopeless.

Christina's call shook Nicolas out of a restless sleep. She told him about a shootout south of Chattahoochee Hills and an anonymous call reporting of forced laborers held captive on a large compound. Nicolas dressed as fast as he could. When he left the house, a limousine was waiting for him to take him to the airport. On the way he called Jason, primarily to inform him about his absence from work. He didn't decline his offer to accompany him to Georgia and made arrangements that Jason would meet with him and Agent Lawry at the airport.

After midnight, the agents were on their way to Whitesburg, Georgia, where they arrived two hours later. The senior agent of the FBI Atlanta department, George Ackerman, welcomed them at the airport. Though he had come in a hurry like everyone else, Ackerman looked wide-awake and as neat as a man leaving a dinner party. Nicolas learned that the senior agent had been attending his mother's seventieth birthday when the information about the gunfight reached him. Like the fifteen agents of the taskforce, he'd packed his equipment and left to meet with the colleagues from DC.

"I understand your involvement," he said to Christina, "but why bring two more agents?"

"I need them to identify at least one of the victims." She tied her hair into a bun and put on the bulletproof vest. "These are Nicolas Hayes and Jason Beckham. They've got a long list of arrests on their account and won't stand in your way."

"Agreed." Ackerman nodded his gray head once.

Nicolas understood he gave them credit but wouldn't tolerate solos. Nicolas could live with that.

They took a large SUV to drive east. Ackerman produced satellite images of the area in question.

"These were taken thirty minutes ago. Looks like the attackers pulled back and left the area after they couldn't get inside." He looked up. "If that was their plan at all."

"What do you mean?"

Ackerman gazed at Christina. "To conquer such a large compound, you need more than a few grenades and rifle power. To me, it looks like a ruse—a shootout that would alert every man to get armed and defend the premises."

"It's also meant to keep them where they are," Nicolas said, curbing his excitement. "Whoever made the call sent those men, too."

"Exactly."

"Who owns the premises?"

"A rich guy named Antony Larkwood. It's a factory with farmlands. According to the trade register, they pack and sell canned vegetables."

"That doesn't explain the attack."

Ackerman shook his head. "I think we're in the middle of a war between two rival gangs. When the attackers learned that they couldn't overwhelm their enemies, they decided to rat them out to the FBI to get rid of them this way."

Jason frowned. "If the defenders are already alarmed, aren't we too few agents to stir up the hornet's nest?"

Ackerman gave Jason a condescending look. "We're the rearguard. HRT, my men, and the Atlanta police are already on site, waiting for my command."

Jason shut his mouth. His embarrassment was the only funny thing Nicolas experienced. Inside, he was as tense as a bowstring and couldn't wait to get to Chattahoochee Hills. If it proved necessary, he would take on the whole gang alone.

Raiden's parents had always been there for him until he reached adulthood. From that day on, so they had explained, he was a master of his fate and could do whatever he wanted. When they decided to leave for Spain with no intention to return, he had stayed, studied naval architecture, and founded a partnership, knowing that his parents were proud of him. He hadn't missed them.

Now he did. He wished he could return to his parents ,like slipping back into a warm cocoon where the real world was miles away and couldn't hurt him.

In his despair, Raiden cursed that he'd ever set foot in Lesley's dungeon. Without his frequent visits, he assumed, he wouldn't have been kidnapped and sold. He couldn't grasp his bad luck. In spite of his ceaseless efforts, he hadn't won Lesley over. She hadn't taken him home or given him any sign that he was welcome in her company. Quite the opposite — she had told him he wasn't any different from other paying customers. She had no feelings in her soul that allowed love to spark. Even if he got out of this misery, no lover waited for him. His parents were far away in Spain. He wondered if anyone had contacted them. He wished they'd never learn of his fate, for he had no hope left that he would find a way to free himself.

However, the look back in time was soothing. His parents were free souls — people who believed in positive thinking and that doing good things prolonged their lives. They had raised their son believing that he was a wonderful individual and that they were chosen to guide him on his way to adulthood. Raiden enjoyed his parents' generosity and support. They possessed enough money to guarantee that he never lacked anything, and yet Raiden preferred to earn his share when he was old enough. Influenced by his parents, he helped the elderly living in a retirement home in his hometown and learned many stories about the past, much more than in any history lesson at school. He learned about the rule of the Third Reich and about how many citizens had fled Germany to escape prosecution. Raiden was grateful for every story, for the more he knew, the more he cherished the peace and the freedom he came to know.

He became an excellent swimmer on the school team, and his parents attended every competition. He wasn't just swimming for the team's success, but also to make his parents proud, and not least, to impress the girls.

So far, Raiden's life had been a string of positive memories, only broken by Lesley's rejection and his subsequent kidnapping.

But now his life was going rapidly south, getting worse from day to day.

The shackles restricted his moves, and the cell was so low he couldn't stand upright. If he hunched his shoulders, he was able to look through the big window into a vast yard that must be beautiful on a sunny day. The yearning for freedom was overwhelming, made more so when he moved his hands and felt the weight of the chains. Judging by the look of the other two victims, he knew that they had lost hope of freedom some time ago. Their gazes conveyed pity. Most probably, they had tried to escape their captors time and time again until the spark of hope was extinguished, together with their will to live. These days, they sat in their cells, listless and with little movement. Though they didn't wear shock collars, they didn't talk. Raiden feared he would look the same in a few days.

His captor served bowls with water and others with food but no cutlery. Treated like this, the three victims in the cells were reduced to animals. Raiden knew enough about psychological manipulation to realize it was but a question of days until he felt and behaved like an animal.

The victim in the cell next to him turned his head. In his eyes, Raiden found nothing but resignation. Like Raiden, he was of impressive physique, with shoulders broad enough to rip apart any jacket. He was blond, and his long hair hung down his shoulders in shimmering waves. The young dude had blue eyes and fair skin, hardly touched by the sun. He wore a black muscle shirt and shorts that were so tight they hardly covered the bulge of his genitals. Raiden assumed that the prisoner was beyond feeling squeamish. Looking closer, Raiden found out that the man's shackles consisted of several rigid parts between his collar and the handcuffs that hampered his movement even more than the chains Raiden was forced to wear. He had to pull his hands under his chest to lower his head toward the bowl to eat. *More like a dog with every day.*

Raiden trembled with renewed fear. *Will that happen to me, too? Will he force me like an animal to take morsels from his hand?* Judging by the short criminal's attitude, he was bound to cow his prisoners until they did everything he wanted. For the life of him, Raiden couldn't eat a bite. His mind ran amok with the images of what his captor might do with him, and his trembling increased until his teeth chattered.

He wished himself away, but the picture that came to his mind was Lesley's beautiful face and the knowledge that she would never be his. The chains around his wrists were clanking when he covered his face with his hands, sobbing in misery.

Nicolas had taken part in missions of the hostage rescue team on several occasions, but every time their precise planning, their weaponry, as well as their timing, impressed him. The armored officers entered the building first, the police forces and the FBI following close behind. The inevitable shootout took thirty minutes, left twelve criminals wounded or dead and sixteen more men arrested by the combined forces. The large atrium smelled of gun powder.

They searched the entire building and freed twenty-two prisoners on three levels as well as twenty men working in the adjacent wing packing canned goods. Nicolas hastened along the cell rows, searching for Raiden and asking the released fighters whether they had seen him. Finally, he came to a Mexican, who sat crying with relief in front of his cell. Upon his question, the man nodded and lifted his head.

"I know who you mean—a man with a long wild mane, right? He's not here. The guards took him away."

"When?"

"Yesterday morning. Yes." He looked up to the ceiling where the first sunlight of the new day shone through. "You missed him by a few hours."

"Do you know where he was taken?"

The Mexican wiped his eyes and looked around, obviously unable to grasp that he was free at last. "He said he was sold to a Chinese man and that he didn't know what waited for him." He made a face of disgust. "Said that it would be worse than dying in a fight."

Nicolas was glad he was already kneeling. His blood pressure dropped so low he was afraid he wouldn't be able to get up again. "Did anyone mention where this Chinese man lives?"

"No. But the guards said something about a shuttle, so he might've been taken away in a car."

"All right." Nicolas got up slowly when Agent Lawry came up to him. "Raiden was taken away, sold to a Chinese man. His whereabouts are unknown."

"Maybe not for long." She looked smug. "We arrested Antony Larkwood, and you won't believe it, but he claims that this is a legal enterprise with every participant having signed a contract to work for him as a gladiator."

Nicolas matched his pace to Agent Lawry's. "Legal? He held them captive and still claims they had contracts? What kind of shit is this?"

Agent Lawry frowned. "The judge has to decide how much of this is BS, but right now, it's important what he tells us while he believes that we'll have him by the balls if he clams up."

Upstairs in the adjacent wing, the furniture and interior design spoke of a man of wealth without the taste to create something worth admiring. It was a stark contrast, though, to the dark and sparsely furnished cells of the inmates he called *gladiators*.

Antony Larkwood sat handcuffed on an armchair and stubbornly repeated that he wanted to call his lawyer. His scarred face was reddened. His agitation gave his voice a hysterical touch. "You can't deny me my lawyer! I have rights!"

"Cut the crap!" Nicolas boomed as he put his hands on the armrests and lowered his face to Larkwood's. "Tell me about Raiden Stroud. Right now! I want to know where you sent him."

"I don't know —"

"You either talk or I'll make you! You had Thomas Zutarski killed. I won't let that happen to Raiden!"

"Thomas is dead? This wasn't my fault! He decided —"

"Where is Raiden?"

"I don't know!" Larkwood looked left and right to the combined forces of HRT and Atlanta Police.

Nicolas understood that his opponent considered himself safe with so many uniformed policemen close by. He hated to play the card at hand. "Get out!" he shouted and turned around to look at the men present. "All of you!"

Agent Lawry was quick-witted and gestured for the uniforms to leave. At last, Jason stood at the closed door like a bouncer, deadpan.

Larkwood huffed. "Don't think you can impress me with your . . . physique. I have — "

"You have nothing!" He reached for the man's hand and pulled his index finger. "I give you one chance to tell me where Raiden was taken."

"And then what? You're gonna break my finger?"

"Exactly. One after the other, your thumbs at last." Nicolas let his words sink in.

Larkwood's scarred face lost its color as he understood that he was in no position to taunt his adversary. "You can't do this," Larkwood said, but with considerable doubt.

"Let me put it like this." Nicolas bent the man's finger toward the back of his hand and enjoyed Larkwood's grimace. "Your enemy ratted you out to the FBI. Yes, don't look like you're surprised. We know of your business because we were told where to find you."

"Bastard!"

"Right on. So you either tell me the whereabouts of the Chinese customer so that I find Raiden, or I'll break your fingers one by one until you tell me of him anyway."

Larkwood howled in pain. "All right, all right! Stop! I'll tell ya!"

Nicolas held tight, unwilling to give in. He wanted to cause that bastard pain and more pain. "Talk."

Larkwood sweated profusely. "He's . . ." His eyes were bulging, and Nicolas eased his grip. "The Chinese man . . . Mr. Cheng . . . he's got a manor . . . in southern Georgia . . . outside Valdosta."

"The address!"

Larkwood complied the moment Nicolas increased the pressure again. Haltingly, he delivered the address of the estate.

Nicolas let go and straightened. Pointedly, he adjusted the

lapels of his jacket. "See? Wasn't that bad, huh? You could've told me right away and spared me the hassle. Or not." He cocked his head. "You had my friend killed, so I should at least leave you with a broken cheekbone." He raised his fist.

"No! I told you what you wanted to know! I told you the truth! You can catch Mr. Wong and his goons. Leave me alone!"

Nicolas hesitated, his gaze fixed on Larkwood's sweaty face. That man had brought so much harm to so many people he deserved being bashed until he bled. Nicolas would still stand trial if he broke his cheekbone and nose.

"Nick . . ."

Jason's voice reached Nicolas through the turmoil of feelings. He wanted to vent his anger on Larkwood. He was the mastermind behind the kidnappings and the mistreatment. He wanted to wreak his rage on him, leave him as a bloody mess and call it justice. That freak had made millions while the victims suffered and died. The image of Thomas's dead body — tortured by a boxer in a knuckle fight until he didn't get up again — was on his mind and wanted to knock out reason. It would be fair — more than fair — to break Larkwood's nose, cheekbone, maybe his jaw, too.

Breathing deeply, Nicolas turned away and passed through the open door where Agent Lawry waited.

"You got what you wanted?"

"We have to pay Mr. Wong a visit in Valdosta. I've got the address."

"Good work. Is he still breathing?"

"Don't ask." Nicolas glanced at her. "I'm not that kind of guy."

She cleared her throat. "I don't know if I would've been able to restrain myself."

CHAPTER THIRTEEN

R aiden didn't understand a word of Chinese, but he could decipher the men's agitation in the corridor and the sudden haste as three guards entered the room, cattle prods at their sides. They fumbled with the key ring, and both victims to the right of Raiden looked up, expectantly. While the guards neglected those prisoners, one of them opened Raiden's cell and ordered him to come out. Raiden hesitated, recoiling from their aggressiveness, but he had no choice. The guards—obviously the strongest of the bunch—grabbed his arms and pulled him out. He wanted to ask a question, but the shock collar prohibited any speaking. Instead, the electric impulse spread through his body like an avalanche and robbed him of his strength. His knees buckled, and he cursed his stupidity. Panting loudly, he absorbed the pain and tried to resist his enemies' attempt at taking him away. The guards grunted and with combined power pulled him toward the corridor and downstairs to the waiting van. Raiden didn't make it easy for them. The men cursed and wheezed until they arrived on the path that was wet from early morning rain.

Hoping against hope to find a way out, Raiden looked around. A black SUV was parking close to the gate with four armed men in black uniforms standing by. Behind it, a long black limousine waited with its engine running. The small Chinese man put his attaché case into the passenger seat. Prior to getting in, he cast Raiden a last, almost loving glance. The limousine and the SUV left the premises at high speed.

186

Raiden was dragged into the van in which he had been transported earlier, locked up, and left alone. Five minutes later, the transporter rolled toward the main street.

Frustrated and in fear, Raiden checked the tethers to see whether he had a chance to free himself and attack the men at their destination. He couldn't break the chains around his wrists, but when he pulled up his legs on the bench and thus had some room with his handcuffs, he could open the carabiner of the thin chain connecting his collar to the wall. Celebrating the small victory, he dedicated the remaining time of the ride to opening the chains between his wrists. He found a protruding head of a hexagonal screw and pushed a chain link over it to stretch it in hope it would burst.

Sweating and with his heart pounding against his ribs, Raiden tried to imagine a reason why he had been taken away while the other prisoners remained. Was the *master* taking him to another abode? Did he intend to show him around? Would he hand him to yet another captor, and this building was nothing but a way station?

He buried his face in his hands and exhaled, rattled by fear of the unexpected.

The helicopters were fast. Yet Nicolas had the impression they were standing still. The idea of losing Raiden as he had lost Thomas was omnipresent and blocked any reasonable thought. No positive word, no encouragement was welcome. Jason understood and left him alone while Agent Lawry praised Nicolas for his clear-headed interrogation and that they were closing in on the last suspect. She considered the possible arrest of the Chinese man and his minions a bonus. The fact that she had solved the case of the kidnapped young men would earn her points with her superior. Though she tactfully tried to hide it, Agent Lawry was very pleased with the results so far.

Jason's gaze was full of worry. He had managed to keep Nicolas from attacking Larkwood but appeared uncertain whether he would have such luck again. Nicolas could tell it wasn't that Jason was concerned that a suspect might be harmed — he was focused on the consequences for Nicolas's career more than Nicolas was right now. Jason would back him up in any decision he made, and yet he would want him to make the right ones and not end up in jail.

If he was honest, Nicolas didn't desire to kill the goons, though smashing their faces might be a relief. He wanted to lock them up the way they had locked up the kidnapping victims and let them rot. It would be satisfying in a gruesome way to see the captors turning into prisoners — to see the fear in their eyes and let them feel the helplessness they had imposed on their victims.

The helicopters touched the ground at last and the local police forces arrived for support. Their captain summed up details about the estate they were going to attack, and the SWAT leader listened carefully. Concerns that this would violate the rights of a foreign citizen were dismissed due to the imminent danger to their prisoners.

The team used thermal imaging cameras to get an overview of the number of enemies in the building and decide on their strategy next. Once more, the FBI agents stood in the second line while the attack was launched.

The Chinese guards at the gate tried to keep the SWAT from entering — claiming it was Chinese territory — but surrendered their weapons without a fight. Realizing that they stood no chance against the overwhelming manpower, the house guards and members of the staff delivered their weapons and were arrested. One of them guided them to the room with the remaining two prisoners kept in cells. Threatened by the presence of Nicolas's and Agent Lawry's service pistols, the guard unlocked the doors and handed the keys to the shackles prior to being taken into custody.

"I can't believe this," Jason mumbled, stunned by the looks of the captives. He gestured to the first man. "Come on, get out. You're free."

The blond man left his prison slowly and carefully, obviously distrusting his luck. He remained on his knees, for the shackles were too tight to let him get up.

"I can't believe this," Agent Lawry whispered, holstering her weapon as she watched the prisoners being freed from their shackles. "How is it possible that men can do this to others?"

"Raiden's not here," Nicolas said, after checking the other rooms. He knelt in front of the blond man, who rubbed his wrists absentmindedly. A part of him was raging mad at what he saw, the other wanted to help undo their misery. "Sir? Do you understand me? What's your name?"

"Kilian." He spoke softly and looked left and right, as if he expected his captor to show up and punish him.

Nicolas was angry, frustrated, and in fear at the same time that they had come too late. He had no explanation why Raiden wasn't with these victims. "Was a third man with you? Tall, with long brown wavy hair?"

Kilian nodded slowly and looked toward the empty cell. "Came here yesterday. He took him with him."

"Who took him?"

"The master." It was a fearful whisper. "The master left the house. He does that from time to time and doesn't come back for a week or two. When he's gone, the guards . . ." He swallowed so hard that his Adam's apple jumped, then shook his head. "They pulled him out of the cell and dragged him away. He didn't want to go with them. But he couldn't say a word."

"He was gagged?"

"Collared." Kilian grimaced as he pointed to his neck. "It's tight and it hurts when you try to speak. We wore it for weeks." He gazed at the open door again. "Until we learned that we were not allowed to speak until spoken to."

A cold shiver ran down Nicolas's spine. He swore he would punish every guard the hardest way possible. "Do you know where Raiden was taken?"

Kilian looked toward the other victim, who sat with his legs drawn up and his gaze fixed on the open door.

"Zac?"

Zac had long black hair and olive skin. Not only was his face shaven to perfection, but — as far as Nicolas could see — his legs and arms, too. Nicolas didn't want to imagine what kind of fetish their Chinese captor preferred. Zac put his chin on his knees and teetered back and forth slowly, gazing into the room without focusing.

"Zac? Did you understand what they were saying? Where were they going?"

Nicolas knew he had to be patient with kidnapping victims. Their trauma was so deep, they were unable to jump up and dance a happy dance about their sudden freedom. They needed time to adjust to the new situation. He couldn't fathom what they had been through, and yet he needed answers.

"Zac, please, we can free Raiden if you tell us what you heard. Did you understand words — anything about their destination?"

Zac hugged himself and buried his face behind his arms. "The master loves beautiful men. Wants them around. Close by. Has a plane. Big enough for his . . . games."

Nicolas exhaled, frustrated, but kept his mood in check. "You think he drove to an airport?"

"We've got something!" The SWAT leader announced from the entrance. "Traffic cameras show a large black limo, an SUV, and a van heading toward the nearest airport."

"He's leaving the country!" Agent Lawry turned on her heels. "How much time?"

Nicolas touched Kilian's arm. "A medic will be here any moment. You'll be taken care of. Do you understand me? You're free at last."

Kilian clearly wanted to say something, but couldn't. He nodded. Tears trickled down his cheeks.

Nicolas wished he could do more, tell him that time would help digest the bad memories, but he had no time. With a last apologetic glance, he turned and ran behind Agent Lawry toward the waiting helicopter.

Raiden heard the roaring engines when the back door of the van opened. A gusty wind tore at his hair as the guards ordered him to get off. Outside, he turned around the door and looked at a smooth white *Gulfstream* with its gangway still open. His fear skyrocketed. He wasn't being taken to another house—the man was about to take him to another state—or country! As the guards grabbed him and pulled him forward, Raiden used his weight and his strength to hamper them. He didn't want to leave the ground for he knew that once the plane was in the air, it would be considered Chinese territory, and no American police force could order the pilot to land.

The guards yelled at him, urged him to walk, but Raiden dropped to the tarmac, struggling with all he had, struggling so hard that the guards called for assistance. At the same moment, the chain between his wrists tore apart. Raiden surprised the guards more than he had anticipated—they looked shocked that a prisoner could do this trick. In the moment of stunned immobility, Raiden kicked out, hitting one of them at the knee so that he dropped away, howling in pain. Sensing a chance for victory, Raiden headbutted the small guy on his left, but he was more resilient than he had anticipated, and then there were two more men approaching from the SUV, pulling out their cudgels. They had a heated and yet clipped conversation while Raiden made every effort to delay entering the plane. So far, they hadn't even crossed half the distance to the gangway, and Raiden was putting up the fight of his life.

A man in uniform stood at the topmost step and gestured for them to hurry.

Raiden understood the word *police* and doubled his efforts to move into the opposite direction, despite four men hanging at his arms and torso. His two hundred and thirty pounds made a difference, even though his feet were still shackled. Adrenalin gave him strength and stamina. He jabbed a guard in the face so that he fell away screaming. When a guard attacked him with his cudgel, Raiden dodged the hit and punched the man's face so hard he dropped the weapon. To his surprise, Raiden caught the cudgel in the air and used it against the next man standing. Still, there were too many enemies to get away from.

Even if he delayed his fate for another five minutes, he would call himself a winner. Once more, the guards kicked and punched him as they tried to break his resistance, and yet, Raiden endured the beating and stood fast against their combined efforts.

A fifth man came running, shouting orders. The goons at his sides grunted with strain, and one of them barked an answer that made the newly arrived one laugh. He pulled a syringe from his breast pocket and uncapped the needle.

Raiden flung himself backward and sent the minions to the ground, spluttering curses.

"ETA?" Nicolas shouted over the clamor of the rotor blades.

Ackerman lifted five fingers and pointed toward the ground. Nicolas's heartbeat accelerated once more. The captor had a lead of thirty minutes at least and could've departed already. He wiped his damp palms on his pants and checked the magazine of his service pistol. It was a habit to calm his mind, but it didn't work.

Ackerman's quick check had revealed that Mr. Cheng was a Chinese businessman with ties to the Chinese government, well protected and independent at the same time. His trade included rare artifacts but also art he lent to museums in the United States for exhibitions. His position resembled the status of a diplomat. If he left in his plane, he was untouchable, for the US government wouldn't start a diplomatic affair about one man kidnapped and deported.

The images of the two victims in their small cells haunted Nicolas as he prepared for landing. Raiden had been one of them — locked up, kept in chains, forced to live like an animal. Though the captives would receive medical treatment and psychological support, they would need a long time to return to their normal lives, if ever.

Ackerman called the airport and demanded that they ground every plane that was waiting on the taxiway. He argued with the airport manager that the FBI was about to arrest a Chinese trader for smuggling and that it was within his rights to close the airport if he deemed it necessary.

Nicolas waited with bated breath until Ackerman gave a thumbs up. "All runways are closed. If the pilot tries to take off, they'll use a fire truck to block it." He grinned, satisfied. "Hey, Hayes, don't look so glum. We're catching the bad guys."

The helicopter descended on the tarmac from a safe distance to the taxi position of a white *Gulfstream*. The moment the helicopter touched ground, Agent Lawry, Ackerman, Jason, and Nicolas jumped out, weapons drawn and ready.

Nicolas felt as if he'd been thrown into a B-movie. On the tarmac and close to a dark gray van, Raiden Stroud was fighting with three Chinese guards in black uniforms, who tried and failed to push him toward the waiting plane. One of them was already limping, the others looked as if they'd fought against a boar and lost. A fourth man struggled to get closer to Raiden's neck, a syringe in his left hand. His face was an unhealthy red, and he shouted at top of his lungs, but to no avail. Raiden shook his head so that his long hair flew from side to side. He dodged the threat with enormous strength and effectiveness.

Ackerman, to the left of Nicolas, was smiled in admiration.

"FBI! Let him go!" Nicolas shouted. "Step away from him and drop your weapons!"

The minions turned in surprise. Raiden used their inattentiveness to shake them off like a dog shakes off water. Quickly, the four agents closed the gap, and the hoodlums realized they couldn't level their weapons faster than they would be shot. Agent Lawry secured the weapons and destroyed the syringe with her boot. While the men were cuffed, the pilot was about to pull up the gateway.

Jason shouted at him to stop. "Get down here and on your knees! If you turn away, I'll shoot!"

Nicolas secured the last thug and turned to Raiden, who appeared to have lost all strength, as if the wires of a marionette had been cut. He slumped to the ground, breathing raggedly, and looking around as if he hadn't expected the fight to end so soon and in such a fashion. When he wiped his face, the chains rattled around his wrists. Getting closer, Nicolas became aware of the collar around Raiden's neck. He suffered a flashback that brought him to his knees.

"Oh god, no." He turned to where Jason handcuffed the pilot to the gateway. "Jason!"

"Coming!"

Behind them, the armored transporters of the HRT arrived and took over securing the criminals and taking them to the waiting vans. No one entered the plane.

"What's wrong?" Jason asked, kneeling.

Nicolas pointed toward Raiden's neck. "Do you remember how to open it?"

Jason pulled out a pocketknife. "Yes." He slipped the blade under the collar. "Just hold still. I know what I'm doing."

Raiden's eyes went wide, but the knife cut through the fibers like cutting through paper. Freed from the restriction, Raiden coughed hoarsely and doubled over.

"Better?" Nicolas asked when the coughing bout was over. He took off his long jacket and helped Raiden put it on. "We'll have the keys to the locks in a moment."

"You came. You found me." Raiden looked close to tears. He shook his head, disbelieving the truth. Suddenly, he laughed, only to sob the next moment. "I don't know how long I could've kept this up."

"Yes, we found you." Nicolas had never before been so relieved to have solved a case. "You put up quite a fight and even burst the handcuffs. That must've been an impressive sight. Looks to me like you didn't need our help."

Jason cast him doubtful glance but didn't say a word.

"I needed your help," Raiden said softly as he glanced at the *Gulfstream* once more. "Sooner than later they would've put me into it." He shivered badly. "I don't wanna know where he'd have taken me."

An HRT member used a skeleton key to free Raiden from the shackles. Raiden pushed the tethers away as if they were snakes out to bite him. Nicolas helped him stand and found himself in a bear hug.

"Thank you. Thank you so much for coming. I thought I was lost."

Nicolas didn't find words but returned the embrace, disregarding Jason's amusement at seeing a bear of a man hug him and Agent Lawry's bewildered look. Raiden's gratefulness moved him deeply, but he was also shaken to the core of having seen yet another man tortured with a shock collar. The memories of his own torment more than three years earlier flooded his mind, and he remembered how Jason had found him in the basement of the serial killer's lair. The sudden bond with Raiden seemed strong and utterly natural. When Raiden let him go, Nicolas took a deep breath to surface from emotions he didn't want to show while on duty.

"We'll take you to a hospital to —"

"What about the other two men?" Raiden's eyes were wide with urgency. "In the cells? Did you find them, too?"

"Yes, we freed them. They've been taken care of."

"Good. That's good to know." Sighing, Raiden ran a hand through his tangled hair. He pointed toward the plane. "What about that asshole on board?"

Agent Ackerman lowered his radio. "Mr. Cheng talked to the Chinese ambassador a few minutes ago. Until that man arrives, he won't leave the plane." He shrugged. "It doesn't matter to me. We arrested Larkwood and his goons, and we stopped Mr. Cheng's illegal activities. Your statement, Mr. Stroud, will make a difference."

Raiden looked up at the plane's still open gateway. "If there's a trial." He scoffed. "I don't see that yet."

"I'm confident." Ackerman walked away to speak with the airport manager.

"Larkwood?" Raiden asked. "He's that scarred guy?"

"Yes. He and his men were arrested, too. We freed all the fighters."

"Really? Wow, that's more good news." Raiden squeezed Nicolas's shoulder. "What about Tom? He told me he knows you."

Nicolas lowered his chin and took a deep breath. "Sorry, but Tom didn't make it."

Raiden took a step back. The pain on his face mirrored Nicolas's feelings of loss and grief. "I hoped I could—I'm so sorry, Nick. So sorry."

"Yes, me, too." Nicolas got a grip and guided Raiden to one of the HRT vans. "But there's good news, too. We'll put away the goons for a very long time."

"That's a reason to celebrate." Raiden got into the van. "I hope you've got some booze hidden somewhere in the car. I could use a good drink."

Chapter Fourteen

Nicolas stayed at Raiden's side during the ride toward the hospital and the examinations. He took care that the young man received warm socks and slippers and took down notes about his state of health and the prescribed medication. While they were together, Raiden shifted between exuberance about his freedom and sadness about how he had suffered.

When they were alone in a waiting room and Raiden couldn't hold back the tears, Nicolas offered him a shoulder to lean on and didn't try to downplay Raiden's inner turmoil with empty words.

Jason arranged for the flight back to DC, a single malt whiskey included. Raiden wanted to go home, told Nicolas he wanted to crawl into a hole and not come out again for a week.

"Hey, I'm really grateful for all that you did for me—not only today. If I have it right, you were involved in the case the whole time."

"Not really. It's Agent's Lawry's case. I trailed along." Nicolas didn't meet Raiden's gaze for fear he would see the sorrow Nicolas carried since learning of Thomas's death.

"Be that as it may. I can't repay you for what you did, ever. But right now, I want nothing more than to go home, take a bath, slip into my own clothes." He laughed, looking down at the apparel Nicolas had given him. "Something more casual than a suit and dress shirt. Don't think I'm not grateful, that's not it. But it's just not my kind of clothing. And then—if I'm lucky, I'll catch some hours of sleep."

"Did the doc give you something?"

"Yes. I didn't want it, but he insisted." He shrugged. "Guess he knows better."

"He does."

"Where are we going?"

"One more stop," Nicolas said leaving the freeway.

"Just take me home," Raiden replied pleadingly. "I can't stand any more strangers."

"Not strangers." Nicolas stopped the car in the driveway of his home.

"Your place, huh? Really, it's kind of you that you want to invite me, and I won't deny that I'm hungry, but—"

"I'm not inviting you. Get out."

Up to the moment the door opened, Raiden looked like a polite guest who wanted to be elsewhere. Then Lesley Gilbert stood at the front door, smiling tentatively. Her face bore the stains of recent tears, but she tried to keep face when it was clear to Nicolas that she would soon cry tears of joy.

"Hello, Raiden. It's so good to see you."

Nicolas could tell that Raiden gave the word *flabbergasted* a whole new meaning, best combined with *dumbfounded, perplexed,* and *thunderstruck.*

"Yeah, well . . . I'm happy to be here. And to see you, too." His body language said he was uncertain whether breaking into a run would be the better alternative than staying.

Lesley turned around, made two steps and turned back with the same tentative smile, as if fearing Raiden would leave to never return.

"I'd prefer to go inside. It's much warmer."

Nicolas gently pushed him toward the living room and once he was inside, closed the door.

Jacklyn came up to him, kissed his lips and whispered, "Let's grant them some privacy."

Raiden's heart hammered — this time not out of fear but out of bewilderment. He kept the question back whether he was meeting the one and only Lesley Gilbert, who had so unmistakably declared that Raiden was just a customer like any other.

"Don't you wanna take off the coat?" Lesley asked.

He could tell she was as insecure as he felt, but the moment of her gentle urging made it easier to take the invitation. He took off the coat and shoes and followed Lesley into the living room. The light was dimmed, and the dinner table set with plates loaded with food. Two glasses and bottles of juice as well as wine were waiting.

Raiden rubbed his beard, too confused to form a coherent thought, let alone words. His mouth was dry, and he poured a glass of juice as he glanced at the dungeon queen as though he hadn't met with her before.

Lesley looked up to him pleadingly. "I think I owe you an explanation. Would you mind sitting down with me?"

Raiden lifted his hands. "Forgive me when I stand here and don't know how to take this. Why are you here?"

"Because I realized the moment you were gone that I can't stand being without you."

He drank and then put his hands on the backrest of a chair. He couldn't have been more surprised if she'd told him she changed professions to become a lawyer. "You pushed me away hard that night, Les. You told me you don't have any feelings for me. Why the sudden change of heart?"

"Because . . . because I lied to you." She blinked away tears as she tried to keep looking into his eyes.

"Lied to me?" Raiden ran a hand through his hair, at a loss how to deal with the situation. If anyone had predicted the turn of events of that day, he would've laughed in his face.

"Please, Raiden, sit down with me. Or do you want to keep a distance?"

"No. Not really." He sat down, and she took his hand, which was a gesture as amicable as it was odd.

"Are you all right?"

While she looked at him with tears in her eyes, he tried to determine an appropriate answer to her question. He was so confused by her sudden friendliness he feared that a wrong word might terminate her kindness and make her leave the house for good.

"I'm okay — some scratches and bruises, nothing serious." He held her warm hand in his, but the belief that Lesley wanted to be touched and that she was staying close to him hadn't yet set in. He wanted to tell her that his time as a submissive in her dungeon was over, but then didn't dare start an explanation that might lead in a direction he didn't want the conversation to go.

"That's good." She frowned, finally understanding his hesitation. "I have so much to tell you and don't know where to start." She made a face. "Or do you want me to leave because we parted on such bad terms?"

"I can't think at the moment, Les, I'm . . . I feel like I've been thrown through a thunderstorm with a small sail, and I don't know whether my boat holds or sinks." He swallowed nervously. "Forgive me that I don't understand what just happened."

Lesley bit her lower lip, nodding, and looking at him with an intensity that was new to him. She appeared to see him as a totally different man — not the one who had tried to get to know her for a year and who had offered his body to punish and to love. She seemed to see beyond the customer of her dungeon and inside the man Raiden had been all along.

"I know this comes as a . . . surprise."

Raiden held his tongue and her hand.

"That night we had a fight I was close to telling you that I would like to see your place. Yes, I know that doesn't sound right or honest in any way. I know that I pushed you away again even though you built me bridges I didn't want to cross. I . . . I can't explain to you the turmoil of feelings you threw me into. The moment you pounded the wall and stormed out of the dungeon, I wanted to call you back and apologize." She caressed his cheek with her free hand. Her voice betrayed her feelings. "I was so close to running after you and begging you to give me one more chance." She sobbed. "And when I finally worked up the courage to follow you, I found your car open, the keys on the ground, and you were gone." She shook her head, weeping quietly. "I've blamed myself for my stupid behavior time and again. I told myself that if I hadn't been such an idiot, this wouldn't have happened." She took a shaky breath. "I shook Nick out of sleep and urged him to help me find you."

"And he did." Raiden bent to touch Lesley's forehead with his lips. It was the first intimate contact he'd dared, and he waited anxiously for her reaction.

"Yes, he did, and I'll be forever grateful." She lifted her chin to meet his lips for a kiss.

Raiden was electrified and felt like he'd been shot into the sky. Not even the awareness of his rescue came close to the high of feelings he experienced now. He wanted it to be real. He wanted Lesley at his side—to share his life with her. However, he had waited for so long for her love to blossom, he couldn't believe with all his heart that she had changed her mind.

They parted, and he looked at her with a feeble smile. "Are you telling me I was close to winning you over?"

"Very close." Lesley lowered her head. "I realized too late that you had already won me over. I wasn't . . . I couldn't understand my own feelings. I was so obsessed with my work at the dungeon and keeping men away from me that I didn't see . . . and didn't understand or cherish what you offered. No man has ever come so close to me."

Raiden squeezed her hand as he whispered, "And you pushed me away, too."

"I know. I was so stupid." Lesley wiped her eyes. "You know the saying — you don't know what you've got until it's gone. I didn't want to think that you might . . . not return." Their gazes met, and they thought of Thomas's murder. "Forgive me when I took you by surprise so badly. I just couldn't wait another day. I had to know right away that you're back."

"Alive and kicking." He managed to smile. Carefully, still thinking she might shy away like a deer, he cupped her face. "And if you want me to, I'll give you a chance. Or two. Or whatever you want."

After Thomas's funeral, Jacklyn and Nicolas drove home in silence.

She had seen Nicolas struggle to return to his former self after being abducted, but his misery back then appeared small compared to the despair he suffered after the death of his friend. His vigor had disappeared and left nothing behind but sadness. Having brought the criminals to justice didn't lift his mood. He claimed he had just done his job. Only the news of Tyrone's death — an obviously cold-blooded killing ascribed to the Mexican gang members — granted him minor satisfaction, but just because the weasel wouldn't harm anyone ever again.

Jacklyn's hopes that Jason's upcoming wedding would improve his state of mind even for a little while were diminished when he mentioned how short Thomas's marriage had been and that his child would grow up without a father. Jacklyn didn't doubt Nicolas wished his fellow agent the best, but he didn't look forward to the ceremony or the party.

When they came home, he changed clothes and went for a

run. He needed solitude to mourn, to think about his life, and to find a way to deal with loss.

As he entered the house afterward, he was overcome with gratitude that she'd understood and left him to his own devices. Unable to find words, he hoped his kiss communicated the depth of his feelings.

At dinner, he told her that Agent Lawry was still looking for five missing men who had been abducted earlier the same year, and that the FBI hoped to find clues to their whereabouts in the many files they had secured at Larkwood's place. She was confident they would free the remaining victims soon and bring their captors to justice. It was no surprise that her promotion was pending by the end of the year.

Nicolas fulfilled his duties as Jason's best man flawlessly. He wore a black tuxedo with a dark green cummerbund, a flower in the jacket pocket, and spit-shined shoes. He had been to the hairdresser and was shaven so smooth Jacklyn had used every occasion to touch his face. By displaying her affection, she had even triggered his smile now and then. When Jason made eye contact, Nicolas gave him a thumbs-up and appeared happy to stand at the altar. However, the sadness in his eyes remained while the church filled with guests. She knew he was remembering Thomas's and Charlene's wedding six months ago and how exuberant the couple had been.

But then came Raiden, and he had Lesley on his arm. As if their appearance restored his belief in goodness and the chance of happiness in life, Nicolas's face lit up. Jason smiled at Jacklyn knowingly. Glad that he'd invited them, she gave him the broadest smile she could manage. She didn't know whether she should be more astonished by Jason's generosity — neither Raiden nor Lesley were his friends — or by Lesley showing up in the most conservative outfit she had ever bought and with Raiden by her side — fully dressed in a tux, with his hair combed back and held by a headband.

Jacklyn looked at Lesley's dark blue cocktail dress that was long enough to cover her knees and the elegant shoes with the usual high heel. She wore matching jewelry — restrained and expensive — and a clutch the color of the dress. When she came up to Jacklyn, she seemed to glow from within. She radiated bliss which did not correspond to her former nature and was — for that reason — even more thrilling. The moment she sat down, Lesley whispered about the assistant at the boutique and how hard it had been to find a dress that wasn't completely boring. Jacklyn was content — her best friend hadn't changed completely.

Raiden appeared to have found his way back to his usual relaxed self. Jacklyn hadn't been surprised to learn that Raiden wouldn't visit the dungeon again — for several reasons. One was that he could now meet with Lesley privately, and another one was the suffering he had experienced in captivity that had changed his view on his lifestyle. Upon Nicolas's urging, Raiden had chosen a psychiatrist to talk to and was confident he would overcome his fears and the reoccurring bouts of depression. He had Lesley at his side, and against her nature she took care of Raiden's daily routines, including his medication and visits to the doc. Jacklyn wondered whether Raiden or her best friend had changed more in the short period of time.

Those reasons set aside, she was happy to see her girlfriend overcome her anxieties and claims that there would never be a man trustworthy enough to let him into her life. Seeing Lesley holding hands with Raiden — her small hand disappeared in his paw — she was confident that together they would explore new ground — even without leather and latex.

The End

Cold Rage
Ann Raina
November 6th, 2020

Even the best intentions have a blind side.

In Richmond, Virginia, Deputy Mayor Dobson is brutally murdered. The FBI investigation reveals that this case isn't the only one in which an abusive husband died of unnatural causes. Special Agent Nicolas Hayes and his team begin the investigation but soon reach a dead end. There is no evidence and no suspect. When an old enemy appears on the scene, the investigation comes to a standstill, and Nicolas finds himself in mortal danger.

Excerpt

Nicolas sipped the coffee while Jason got the keys to their car. "What's so important that you called me in the middle of the night?"

"Deputy Mayor Dobson of Richmond was murdered yesterday morning. Richmond PD was at the crime scene first, but then their chief decided they'd better drop the file onto our desk. I can't tell if someone put pressure on him, but now it's our case."

"Okay." Nicolas slipped behind the wheel and put the mug into a holder. "What took them so long? Internal quarrels we should know of?"

"No. Dobson's bodyguard called the police yesterday in the afternoon and—"

"In the afternoon? Didn't you just say the mayor was murdered in the morning?"

Jason grunted in his beard. "If you'd let me finish, it'll become clear." He held his breath and the door handle as Nicolas gunned the engine and the sedan roared up the slope toward the street. No matter what level of urgency, his partner was addicted to speed like a race car driver. "Dobson's bodyguard, Victor Morrison, reported the crime when he woke up. He stated he'd been knocked out by some kind of gas from a spray can. He found his employer beaten to death in the living room of the house the deputy mayor was being shown around by a real estate agent. The woman's description has already been sent to police stations in the districts. They're searching for her."

"Knocked out by some kind of gas?"

"Morrison stated he was about to follow Dobson and the lady when he was hit by the gas. Dobson wasn't affected, and Morrison went down so quickly he can't tell what happened next."

"Shouldn't he have entered the next room first?"

"That might be so, usually, but it didn't happen in this case."

ABOUT THE AUTHOR

Ann Raina lives and works in Germany with cats and a horse. Riding and writing are her favorite hobbies. So far, she has written twenty-five novels for eXtasy Books with more to come. Twisted Mind, Her latest series,
starting with *Twisted Mind*, deals with FBI Agent Nicolas Hayes, his cases of capital crimes, and his demanding and commanding lover, Jacklyn Hollander.

In all of her books she combines romance, suspense, and humorous elements, for no thrilling story can stand without a comic relief.

For contact turn to annraina@yahoo.com

On Facebook https://www.facebook.com/ann.raina.7

www.ingramcontent.com/pod-product-compliance
Lightning Source LLC
Chambersburg PA
CBHW070831120626
46556CB00002B/717